Samuel Jackson Gardner

Autumn leaves

Samuel Jackson Gardner

Autumn leaves

ISBN/EAN: 9783337374297

Printed in Europe, USA, Canada, Australia, Japan

Cover: Foto ©Andreas Hilbeck / pixelio.de

More available books at **www.hansebooks.com**

AUTUMN LEAVES.

BY

SAMUEL JACKSON GARDNER.

NEW YORK:

PUBLISHED BY HURD AND HOUGHTON,

401 BROADWAY, CORNER OF WALKER STREET.

1865.

CONTENTS.

CONTENTS.

AUTUMN LEAVES.

THE NEW YEAR.

HOW odd it is that the first month of the New Year, which will come in to-morrow as punctually as the Sun, — the youngest of the twelve sisters, — should be figured as an old man, one Aquarius, with a long flowing beard, and likewise a long water-pot and flowing water. He looks almost as ancient as Father Time himself, and might easily be mistaken for that old gentleman, if he had an hour-glass and scythe, showing his occupation to be to mow down the grass, while our friend Aquarius has been, certainly ever since we saw him in the Almanac a great while ago, perpetually employed in irrigating the clover to make it grow.

Strange, how remarkably well the world bears its age ; the last New Year looked as fresh and comely as it did in the time of Methuselah, — we will not say of Adam, because of that we are not quite certain, — and there is not the least doubt that to-morrow will have as few wrinkles in her face as any preceding New Year's Day, at whatever age of the world. Though Time is as old as the hills, yet a day, which is part of it, is as fresh and youthful as the flower that will bloom in June upon the mountain-side. Just so with that other piece of antiquity, the Ocean, which has sometimes even been taken as a symbol of eternity. It must therefore be allowed to be venerable enough; and still the little white-capped waves, that run up in the sweet summer morning to kiss a child's bare vermilion toes upon the hard sandy beach, are as young and frolicsome as any infant of them all. Men and women may be old to-morrow, — at least the men may, — older than they were ten years ago; but the rosy hours of the day itself may and ought to be to them as joyous, new, and full of vivacious thoughts as their little tricksy grandchildren.

Some think that the New Year preaches, and so they go to preaching also. I shall do no such thing. That is the business of the Old Year; so that part of the service will be considered to be over. The singing comes next. That is humbly conceived to be the true office of New Year's Day. The New Year sings. When shall a man ever sing, if not when another year has come, and he finds he is alive, and as happy as may be, in the possession of troops of friends, more or less real, as the experience is. For this let us rejoice and sing; it is no time to be sad. Has there been sorrow in the year that is gone? That is dead, and let the dead bury its dead, and its sorrows with it. The New Year is full of fruition and of hope; like the young orange-tree, it bears fruit and blossoms at the same time.

The remarkable spectacle of the rising up of a whole sex, and bowing down before another — to woman, is proof of a celestial power beyond the mandates of a statute-book. No more need to enforce an observance of woman's rights, where such respect is voluntary, than it would be for legislatures to reënact the laws of nature. Nor is this feminine prerogative limited to the first day of the year. To make it lasting, men assemble, then, in the drawing-rooms of the fair, and enter into a covenant, sometimes, they do say, sealed with a kiss, that the allegiance pledged at that time shall be continued throughout the rest of the year. For this purpose good care is taken to have their names recorded in a book, so that they may be charged with various gallant duties during the succeeding months. In this proceeding there is a strong resemblance to the customs of the Jews in the reign of Augustus Cæsar, who went up at a stated period to Jerusalem to be taxed. In the modern practice the taxes enacted are of the most agreeable description, not confined to money-matters by any means, though these are not neglected, but comprehending the obligation of gratifying pleasant feminine desires, commands, and caprices of all sorts and kinds, in all places and times. How much more delightful and really valuable this undisputed sway, spontaneously accorded, than to have the world's dirty political drudgery forever upon their hands!

The custom of renewing sentiments of regard and gallantry to the other sex on the first of January, we take to be a relic of the old spirit of chivalry, which required the utmost deference to ladies on all occasions, and a firm resolution to defend them from all manner of wrong. This, be it understood, is the implied obligation of all men who make visits on the New Year. " Why, this is a very serious business, really; we must be sober, Jack." " Certainly you must, dear Sir. Intoxication on New Year's is suicide, or flat burglary at least. Take care, for on this day frequently appears that famous *first glass* which, when offered by the hand of beauty, and recommended by her seductive voice, has slain its tens of thousands. Dash it from the lip."

There could never have been a period when a point of time corresponding with our New Year was not an occasion of rejoicing. A time must have once existed when men became alarmed at observing the gradual recession of their only source of light and heat. Before astronomy had revealed the knowledge of the revolutions of the planets, apprehension must at this season have seized upon the minds of all that the sun might possibly abandon the earth entirely to eternal frost and darkness. An exultation, then, must have been experienced in some proportion to their previous fears, upon observing him at length first pausing in the winter solstice in his passage to the south, and then beginning gradually, as he had retired, to return to the abodes of men. So wonderful an event as this must have impressed all minds with the profoundest awe, which even the annual repetition of the phenomenon for six thousand years to the view of men has not had the power entirely to extinguish.

The Old Year and the century preceding it have left us a noble inheritance. If we have the spirit of grateful heirs, and not of the juveniles of the *rising* generation, which is in danger of spoiling like sour beer by excessive fermentation, the estate may be much augmented. But, somehow or other, it always happens, that, in spite of the improvements and inventions of the century, humanity seems not destined to elevate itself much above its present sphere any more than it has been able to add a cubit to its stature.

Notwithstanding the accumulation of ingenious discoveries and contrivances, the lever essential to lift them from the level where their original faculties have placed them seems not to be among the machines yet patented at Washington. The world lags far behind its hopes and prophetic visions. Performance does not proceed parallel with expectation.

We are perpetually slipping from the ladder on which we are attempting to ascend. One would suppose that the acquisitions of every year and century, if properly improved and added to the common stock, would swell the powers and capacities of the race to the limit of theoretic calculation. But hypothesis is sobered down by fact, and it is found that man does not grow better or wiser with any greater rapidity than he grows richer. So Dr. Price indeed long since proved that a penny put at compound interest at the Christian Era would have amounted long ago to the value of a lump of gold many times larger than the earth! The powers of arithmetic are evidently superior to those of human nature. Every man unfortunately has to begin where Watt and Newton did, and three or four generations will record no growth, though they probably will a dissipation of the golden lump of the Astors. If one would commence where they left off, and every generation could stand on the shoulders of its predecessor, human nature would ascend. As it is, it takes a lifetime to learn to do as well and think as well, and know as much as those who have gone before us, and carried away with them almost all that made them what they were. What they have left behind is comparatively little beside their own example, and such odds and ends as are always abandoned upon removals from one residence to another. In this way it is as much as each generation can perform to get possession of the capital of human acquisition and preserve it, so that little time or ability is left to add any interest, according to the theory of progress, to the principal. It is even more than nations have done heretofore to preserve the principal without loss. Such a disaster has several times occurred in history, and the invention of printing seems the only security which we have even now, that similar catastrophes shall not occur again.

As New Year is a famous holiday, it *does* seem singular that one of the very shortest days, and, we may add also, likely to be one of the coldest of them too, should be hit on in which to celebrate it. In this respect the thing was better managed, if it existed, when the year by common consent commenced in March, as was the case just previous to the time of Addison and Steele, as the old editions of the "Spectator" will testify to their scientific reader. But what with the reformation of the Calendar by

Gregory, the English statute law, and the precision of the equinoxes, plain people will, by and by, not be able to decipher the season of the year at all. The learned in such matters already assure us, that, as the dog-days ages ago occurred in June at the heliacal rising of the Dog-star Syrius, so ages hence they will for the same reason happen in October. About that time, too, we shall no longer look for the North Pole to the cynosure in the tail of the Little Bear, but somewhere in the neighborhood of Vega in the constellation of the Lyre. This is perfect truth, notwithstanding the last suspicious word. Then, and not till then, as we fear, will take place that happy era of good feelings, so much longed and looked for, when Americans will know no North nor South, but rejoice in felicitous ignorance both of the points of the compass and of sectional dissensions.

But, as has been said, the anniversary of the year's nativity happens now in the dead of winter in this latitude, and it becomes us, therefore, to make the best of it. And does not everybody try with all his might to do so? No one can doubt this fact, who observes the desperate efforts made by many to be happy, or make believe so. If they *do* economically pick the shortest day in the year to be merry in, can anybody take more trouble to make a pain of pleasure than they do? They borrow of the night to increase its length, and swallow terrible bitters to render it sweet. If it is impossible actually to augment the number of the holiday hours, many succeed entirely in making them and other things appear double, by a suitable and judicious application of the " Original Packages."

But the future, — the obscure, the distant, the uncertain, hopeful future, — what of that? It possesses a very different coloring for the young and for the old. The pencil of Titian, dipt in heaven's rainbows, would not paint it in hues so brilliaht as imagined by the fancy of the one, nor that of Buonarotti, in shadows deep enough to equal the gloomy apprehensions which sometimes cloud the minds of the other. The past of a long life may be affirmed to be a remarkably pleasant contemplation. But note this, — *the past of the old man is the future of the youth ;* the sad or sober experience of the one is what the bright hope of the other is made of, for it was once his own. Such are the materials, young man, from which anticipations of happiness are woven. Beautiful embroideries are they ; but as the richest lace-work covers aching bosoms, so are these airy webs of hope ever inviting us onward, but almost always fade, if they do not vanish on their approach. He who expects least, we believe, generally enjoys most ; and this is a reward and encouragement for moderation equally in business and in pleasure.

LIBERTY.

O, Liberty!
What savage fire thy face is flushing!
And see! thy hands with crimson blushing,
    Bloodshot thine eye!
Gods! must thou come forever rushing
With massacre and madness, crushing
    Those thou wouldst free?

O, Liberty!
'T was ever thus, in classic ages,
From bold Thrasybulus through pages
    Of history,
Man's rights, ne'er won by saints nor sages,
Were earned, the bitter blood-wages
    Of victory!

O, Liberty!
Exiled to catacomb, or manger,
Spurned through the universe, a stranger,
    Or enemy;
Thy native element is danger;
Thy awful office, the avenger
    Of slavery!

O, Liberty!
Up! up! The victim's on the altar;
Doubt not and tremble not, nor falter,
  Beyond the sea;
Nay! With no double purpose palter;
Fear nothing — guillotine nor halter;
  'T is destiny!

O, Liberty!
America, the age's wonder,
The crash of revolution thunder,
  And battle-cry, —
Rending old monarchies asunder,
Avenging centuries of plunder, —
  Shall pass you by!

O, Liberty!
The angel, which the earth is smiting,
Upon your doors, in bloody writing,
  The sign shall see, —
Red symbol of your sire's inditing,
For life and independence fighting, —
  And from you flee!

O, Liberty!
At length the long-expected morning
Of risen humanity is dawning:
  Pray God it be!
The bow of hope the sky 's adorning,
Though lingering clouds still mutter warning
  To tyranny!

O, Liberty!
Won by our sires in battles gory,
They left us freedom crowned by glory,
Their legacy!
Set it, brave countrymen, before ye,
In stone, on canvas, and in story;
It shall not die!

THE MAN OF INDEPENDENT OPINIONS.

HE man of independent opinions feels himself of great consequence on that account,
taking full as much pride in their independence as their correctness. He holds on to them
with obstinate tenacity, not because they are true,
but because they are his. He flatters himself that
so tight a hold of a thing argues strength. And so
it does; but of what ? Of understanding ? Not
always, any more than the grip of a vice proves it
to have a powerful mind. It may be temper, it may
be doggedness, it may be, like the vice, the grip of
a double blockhead.

A man of independent opinions is severe in his
judgments. Not content with pronouncing another
to be wrong, he is apt to think, and sometimes says,
that he is not only wrong, but knows it. He
charges him with being criminally erroneous; err-
ing on purpose and with bad motives. If any one
is what he calls independent in his sentiments,
which, according to him, very few are beside himself, it is accepted as proof of correctness. He

desires in fact no better evidence of another's infallibility than that he differs from almost everybody else. ' Believing the right way to be always narrow, he cannot be complimented as a person of broad and generous sentiments ; on the contrary, though strong, they are contracted. Indeed, he grasps things with such a force as to crush or dwarf them with the very violence of his approval.

It is sometimes remarked, that he of independent opinions is conspicuous for integrity ; that he is more honest than other people. Gruffness and grossness pass with some for sincerity, while suavity is held suspicious. But there is often to be found quite as much of the cat beneath the lion's hide as under the lamb's. Integrity is not a thing of manners, nor even of the temper. It is not a thing at all, but a principle of the moral sentiments quickened into life and action by the warmth of the heart. It may reside within him who was born to differ, but just as likely too in the man who is inclined by nature to agree.

It must be admitted that the usefulness of the man of independent opinions is not remarkable. A sort of innate contrariness renders him an odd stick, that makes it impracticable sometimes to work him into the social edifice. He will not keep parallel with the rest of the timber, nor exactly perpendicular either ; nor cut precisely any of the conic sections, so that calculations may be made upon him. He will see just as he pleases, and no otherwise; and so he is not of so much value as his really good qualities would seem to adapt him to be. But if there happens to be a great deal of him, he may do something all alone by himself, as an advance-guard, or forlorn hope in society.

There are numerous counterfeits or affectations of this species of independence. They are as disgusting as they are impudent. One who has never had any social position, or has lost it, can lose no more by coming out from the crowd and setting up for himself. Having found that thinking and acting very much as others do has not paid, he resolves on trying what differing will effect for him. He protests against this and that, calls in question principles that have been settled ever since the flood, and dresses up his crude, superficial notions into quite a specious sort of philosophy, at least for the million. If he is a politician, he dashes away, like Junius in malignity, not in grace or genius, at the miserable men who happen to have the misfortune to be in office. Nothing they do for the interior or exterior of the country, nothing they spend or save, — whatever they do or omit, — escapes his censure. He is up to them, down on them, and into them. No age, no acquirements, no genius or celebrity, not death itself, can awe him. He speaks his independent thought right out, freely, hit or hurt whom it may, contradicting the greatest authorities and names — his own among the rest — once at least every day. Why not? Should not a man be independent? Should he be afraid of anybody, or chained by slavery to a man, a party; to consistency or truth ? — No.

And as he deals with sentiments, so with motives. " The conduct of the government is unprecedented and mistaken," he says ; but that is nothing, unless he adds, " it is also flagitious and corrupt." " The course which a high officer has seen fit to pursue has been purchased by the grossest bribery." " The Senator from ⸺ would not have expressed such sentiments, if he had not been tampered with, and it is easy to see by whom." " The editor of ⸺ knew, when he wrote the words we have quoted, that he lied ; — he never mistakes, but always falsifies."

Your man of independent opinions is thus seen to be independent also in his speech and conduct. In fact, he is, as he assumes, the only one who is so, and is consequently entitled as of right to deal his freedoms about with no regard to character either of himself or others. There is but one animal known in nature hereabouts, we believe, that is armed with a fluid which renders it terrible, because it is hateful to all others, and obtains its advantages by its ability to excite disgust instead of dread. It gains its point by making itself an object, not to be feared, but shunned. Has this odious creature any likeness to the MAN OF INDEPENDENT OPINIONS?

2

CONVERSATION.

CONVERSATION is the act of interchanging ideas by familiar speech or discourse. There must then be two persons at least to carry it on, and the communication of thoughts must be free and unrestrained. Another ingredient in the definition is, that there must be ideas, sentiments, thoughts. There is no difficulty in any part of the definition but this; and here confession is to be made, that a question may arise as to its correctness. If one were to find out what conversation actually is by listening, he would, of course, leave thoughts out of the definition, as people leave them out in their practice. But we venture to incorporate them in deference to ancient tradition.

Conversation is not a speech, nor a series of any such wire-drawn expansions of dulness. Neither is it twattle about books, nor story-telling. Some men, when an idea is struck out by an interlocutor, which happens to hit their cranium, instead of sending it back with interest, instantly fall into a reminiscence, and begin to narrate what a certain man said to him on a certain occasion, or what occurred to himself on another. By the time this pedlar of old wares gets to the end of his narrative, the spontaneous stream of talk has been dammed up. The shuttlecock has been suffered to fall by the bungling player, and now the game is at an end, or must be set on foot again by some one who can " keep robin alive." Hence the nimble-witted conversationist is known as the life of every party.

There is a graceful skill in fine conversation, and women have it in perfection, as far as its machinery goes. How rapid the motion of the wheels so well lubricated and so easy, — but, alas, for the grist! With a gentle, voluble, and most agreeable clatter, sometimes rising into sounds like drops of honey falling on bells of silver, how charmingly the notes of female conversation come to the ear! Pity, they should sometimes reach no further. If conversation were song, what music should we have? But it is not sound exclusively, however the general practice would make one believe it to be.

There are exceptions among women, as among men. Not all, by any means, suppose the conversation to be this trivial, empty thing. Yet fine talk is certainly rare, and the few examples of it in the intercourse of even cultivated men are sufficient to create a suspicion, or a hope at any rate, that men are prosers in the parlor, because, like Adam Smith, they are saving their ideas for their books. Otherwise, it is difficult to account for the multitude of men whom we are taught to look upon at a distance as wits and scholars, who turn out to be, across the table, merely witlings and pedants.

Men, however, have a title to be twattlers in talk, and bores in letter-writing. Their brains are put every hour almost to such hard scullion and mill-work as to be incapable, even under the lash of other peoples' wit, of getting out of the draught-horse gait. But the gentle, the sensitive, and magnetic sex — why should their ethereal spirits effervesce and exhale into invisible air, without leaving anything substantial behind? Conversation is, and should be, their empire, where they do, and ought to, sit upon the throne. Aye, and do they not, like other princesses, seek to weigh these rather by the Divine right of the physical beauty they inherit than of mental charms of their own acquisition? We do not make the accusation, but may we not to some extent lament, that woman should not occupy and adorn the sphere first assigned her of leading and shining in conversation, instead of declaiming and expounding in the market-place and forum, where she can neither lead nor shine?

Women might be at home in this skilful act of fence, — in the pungent, not venomous sally, the quick retort, — in the suggestive remark, which being the birth of the moment, seems like inspiration, — the beautiful sentiment, and pathetic touch of feeling, — not excluding gentle satire, pointed, yet polite, — in keen, though courteous, criticism. She might be admired for her raillery, if without railing; learned she might be as an Aspasia or De Stael, if not overloaded. Eloquence even might be forgiven in the conversation of the fine woman or sensible man; but it will be tolerated only when it cannot be helped, as it bursts out spontaneously and unawares, not staying to put on the stiff brocades and lace ruffles of full-dressed rhetoric. Your set rhetorician, tricked out in all his finery and pretension, is an abomination in the domestic circle, and a scarecrow to conversation, frightening away not only that unwelcome bird, but scores of little chirpers and songsters, that help to harmonize and diversify the general chorus.

Women, however, are not chargeable with this fault, though some are beginning to try and see if they cannot prose and preach and be as dull as men. When they have once established their equal claim, they will be also rewarded, as men are, with indifference, contempt, and neglect. Insipidity is the rock of the fair sex. Gossip is good in its place; but that place is in the kitchen. Its essence is frivolity when it is not detraction. It is a dish of bitter herbs served up with sharp acids — provocative of an appetite for calumny. Gossips somehow or other have come to be considered of the feminine gender, we believe. The lexicon and observation tell a different tale. Some of the arrantest of the genus have been and are men, who impart to petty talk a harshness, and sometimes poison, unknown, it is hoped, to female lips. Gossip of that base sort becomes a traitor, conspiring against the peace of a neighborhood or circle, instead of a ridiculous trifler and *quidnunc*, and therefore ought to be hated and exterminated — not simply tolerated, laughed at, and despised.

Though we have thus had our little gossip about conversation, the delightful but much-abused entertainment of so many hours, — the want of which is more to be regretted than that of either riches or honors, — and have not attempted to *discuss* the subject, yet we cannot think of concluding without entering a protest against making it the vehicle of slander, immorality, irreligion, or lies of any sort. Conversation must be always pure, even if it is poor. Never is it so thoroughly despicable and mean as when it treats virtue and good men with gibes and scoffs, in order to let off a pun, or tickle the ear with a sarcasm. Ill-temper is bad enough in private intercourse, in all conscience; but the baseness of hurting another's feelings, or damaging a good cause from the miserable vanity of showing off a talent one imagines he possesses, far transcends any epithets of abhorrence we can now apply to the offence.

It may be observed that nothing has been said against the vices of flattery and compliment. The reason is, that our national proclivity is not to a profusion of compliments, and so little danger exists of its excessive indulgence.

GOOD–NATURE.

 SWEET and amiable temper constitutes a more attractive element of character than do the most precisely correct principles. We are not disposed to stop now to quarrel about the relative merit of the two. Some will say, no doubt, that a benignant, genial disposition is God's donation, and that principles of strict and systematic accuracy are our own acquisition; that we are indebted for the one; for the other, on the contrary, entitled to much credit. We neither acknowledge nor deny; we hate to be always giving reasons, as much as Falstaff did. Ethics shall decide the matter any way; provided there shall be left to us the liberty of loving the good-tempered person, and only respecting the other.

The other day we happened to fall in with a casual specimen of a good-natured gentleman. He had some time before been unjustly treated, as he thought, by another person in a negotiation; and was accordingly, though of a happy temperament, considerably incensed. Mr. A. (so we will call

him) resolved never to hold intercourse again with
the man who had offended him ; and he said so.
Mark how the flint carried fire. About a month
afterwards, a friend, acquainted with the circumstance, received a note from him, recommending
the person who had done the wrong to a lucrative
situation in the bank where he was one of the di-
rectors. The friend was much surprised of course ;
and a day or two afterwards, meeting Mr. A., inquired " how he came to be exerting himself in
benefiting an enemy against whom he had vowed
revenge." He opened his eyes, and seemed just
waked up to a consciousness of the position of
affairs. " Why, to confess the truth," said he, " I
did not recollect that little circumstance at all.
The next time I have a quarrel to revenge," he observed, with a smile, " I must take care to make a
memorandum of it." We shall not much fear the
spite of a gentleman who has to write it in a note-
book, lest he may forget it. Let us all show our
indignation at injuries done us, by aiding the wrong-
doer to obtain employment. If such advice is
taken, we cannot answer for the consequences.
One will be, in all probability, to do away with a
great many anti-societies ; which, we take it, is an
abbreviation of the antipathy-societies.

FALSE ESTIMATE OF MEN.

T is a dangerous mistake that we fall into unawares when we attribute to an individual a capacity for some particular thing, because he is seen to possess a faculty for another particular thing. The error is not the less in fact, because there is a specious show of logic to uphold it. A clergyman, for example, lends his name to a certificate of the virtues of a nostrum; or, still more ambitiously perhaps, to an entire theory of medicine. Or, a physician pronounces with similar presumption on the merits of a dictionary, or a point of constitutional law.

Now, every man is entitled to his opinion on every matter beneath the sun, and to talk like a fool, if he chooses, concerning things beyond and above that luminary, as some have lately done, I fear, about the planet Neptune. Men who have come, somewhat late in life, into the possession of their fortunes, (in consequence of being obliged to earn them first,) may talk with ludicrous pretension at the head of their tables

about the different vintages of their wines, and the
merit of their pictures, as if success in business
brought them learning as well as luxury. This is
not the trouble. The misery is, that what such
men assert is felt unhappily to possess a weight, of
which it is not by any means deserving. The
sophistry is here. The clergyman has probably
convinced the public, at least a portion of it, that
he understands the laws of Deity and of our moral
nature ; and is skilful in discovering remedies appointed for their violation ; *therefore* he must be
equally knowing, especially as he is frequently
styled doctor, in relation to that of health, and the
treatment of disease. What a palpable *non sequi-
tur!* It is more : it is a flagrant perversion of the
reason. And how in the other instances mentioned,
do the laws of physiology, current among the faculty,
help them to an acquaintance with those of States
and nations, or to a critical analysis of language ?
Or is there anything in the process of digging gold
in any country, which of necessity refines and
elevates the taste ? These are all abuses of the
understanding, quite as real as the cup and balls of
Signor Blitz, and attended with all the charges of
deception without any of its pleasure.

The truth is, that strong faculties, unlike misfor-
tunes, which are said rarely to come single, are
hardly ever found in clusters ; never in such pro-

fusion as to warrant the inference of the possession of one power of the mind merely from the presence of another. And yet, unfortunately, from the very limited amount of information we can commonly obtain about our fellow-creatures,— and it is meagre indeed among all of us, who are not phrenologists nor clairvoyants, — this, in a vast variety of cases, is the only expedient left to decide upon the capabilities of each other. We have occasion for a family physician; how shall we select him? By advising with another of the faculty? That *would* be droll indeed. And what do the rest of the wide world know of the medical qualifications of any youthful Galen? There is obviously no other method than to catch your candidate in a corner, and cross-examine him on matters on which you pretend yourself to have some knowledge. If, as is likely, you happen to know nothing, the case is manifestly desperate.

On the contrary, should it be your rare goodfortune to be acquainted with anything whatever, as, for instance, the question of liberty and necessity, if your Æsculapius should be as flippant and as shadowy as the profoundest and obscurest metaphysician could desire, still he may be wofully deficient in observing power, sagacity, and fertility of resources in emergencies; and so, after all, though able to thread his logical way through Locke and Edwards, Hume and Kant, he may be gravelled by the first dubious symptom he may chance to encounter in the art of healing, and consequently be a miserable physician with all his dialectics. So a politician — and this is as true as unheeded — may hold forth eloquently on public questions, without the ability to carry the least of them into effect by judicious legislation; and a parent of good preaching talents may lay down most beautiful rules for the regulation of families, and miserably fail in the application of every one of them to his own. In short, Newton's opinion of an epic poem might in all likelihood have been hardly worth the asking; and Daniel Webster, it is possible, would have been considerably posed had he ever tried, as I don't believe he ever did, to write an entertaining novel.

With the exception, then, of universal geniuses, if such creatures ever lived, whose intellects seize many, though not quite all, subjects with gigantic grasp, a man ought to thank the stars if he possesses one faculty rising above the surrounding level of dull mediocrity.

Assuming this discriminating and sober estimate of the capacities of mankind, the difficulty recurs of using men according to their individual and appropriate gifts. The mastery of a single tool gives wealth to a mechanic and fame to an artist. But to ferret out the master-faculty of a man, the most wonderful of all machines, and employ it to advantage, requires a talent belonging only to men of superior discernment. Some conquerors and despots are celebrated for this force of insight, but it is pretty apparent every day, every *election*-day at least, that in countries where the people are the sovereign they will be principally remarkable for oversight in this particular.

Forgetful of these obvious facts, we assume some developments of the intellect to be exponents of its general powers — at any rate as indications of the capacity we are in pursuit of — when, if we investigated deeper, we ought rather to suspect that the presence of one might be owing to the absence of the other. There is no faculty, perhaps, more calculated to engender error in our judgment of each other than the fascinating one of oratory — the fluent extemporaneous preaching power. This is not the proper place to assign the philosophical reasons for this remark, yet it must be said that volubility is in general a very equivocal evidence indeed of strength of thought or efficiency in action. The history of men who have imprinted their signet on the ages, is demonstration of this assertion. Still the noisy rhetorician passes himself off now, as he did at Athens in the time of Cleon, for a competent successor of a Pericles; and a credulous and gaping public, believing that he who can master a multitude of words can command of course a regiment of men or direct the councils of a cabinet, is simple enough in every age to trust him with the baton and portfolio.

I had concluded to end this subject here, till some future time at least, when an incident arose upon my memory, showing what a fog we often look at one another through. One day a mechanic-looking person presented himself before me, together with a model, requesting my opinion of the elements of success rapt up in his invention. It proved, upon inspection, to be " a machine for splitting hides" to the last degree of attenuation. I was not a little puzzled to conjecture what he saw in a gentleman of the long robe to induce him to repose confidence in my advice respecting the qualities of a tool which did not appear to have marked connection with the statutes of the State, or the laws of nature or of nations.

Notwithstanding some misgiving, still I proceeded to examine the unknown novelty with deliberate gravity, but said nothing. After discharging divers knowing looks and inarticulate sounds, and showing other indications of intelligence familiar to gentlemen of all the learned professions, I believe, I pronounced decidedly in favor of the applicant, and pocketed the usual fee. Since then, it has been a source of much comfort to me to learn that the public, the great court of appeal in all cases of this sort, has confirmed the decision which I made. This was confidently anticipated, but I have never since been quite clear about the motive which influenced the honest man to consult a lawyer on the subject. I suppose it was, however, that he thought he could not possibly apply to a better source for counsel about a machine for splitting hides than to a member of a profession distinguished through all lands for unparalleled ingenuity in splitting hairs.

SPRING.

"It comes in smiles and tears; looks in a-tiptoe
  At our vine-draped windows; wakes us up
  With the fly's first hum, and the music of young leaves;
  Rouses the old sap in age's sleepy veins,
  And fills breasts, yet in the milk of youth, with hope,
  Which, like a fluttering mother-bird, flies just
  Before them, tempting them by guile away
  From home's sweet nest, from comfort and repose." — MS.

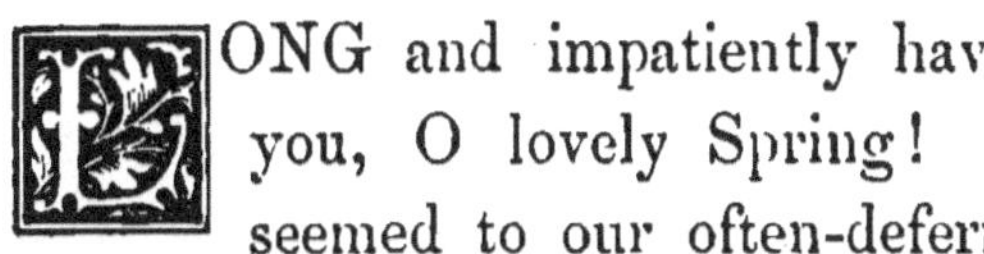ONG and impatiently have we waited for you, O lovely Spring! Ah! you have seemed to our often-deferred hopes a terrible laggard during the dark cold months that we have been anxiously looking for your coming, prinked out in daffodils and crocuses, and young green grass. Oh, how we have longed to smell their delicious odors, and inhale your balmy breath, and the sweet scents of the genial, steaming earth, veiled in a dreamy mist, as if not quite awake yet from its long, long winter's sleep! But you have indeed come at last, dear Spring; and I will be happy, and think of nothing but joy. I will not whisper a reproach, that you have been dallying like a faithless beauty with other admirers for three quarters

of the year, and drinking in their sighs and praises, as you now do mine. Oh! you false one! How often have you broken your solemn promises, and the hearts also that trusted in you! Yet, infatuated that we are, we clasp you, at each return, with irrepressible ardor to our breasts. Those truthful gentlemen, the poets, have told us of your caprices, and we have ourselves seen Winter (shame upon your taste!) sometimes " lingering in the lap of May "; yet have we still weakly continued to confide in your fidelity. It grieves me though, dear Spring, that you should introduce yourself with such windy professions as you do; but a few April tears and warm glances will soon, I dare say, melt our hearts, so that we cannot help forgiving all your peccadilloes, were they twice as many as they are. In the mean time, however, one hardly knows when to congratulate himself on your approach, so dubious, often, is your appearance, any more than the proper time to laugh when some persons are trying to execute a joke. I must think, indeed, my pretty Spring, that you yourself are sometimes little better than a sorry jest.

But I promised not to play the critic. Still, would that you had come sooner! The poor, sinking invalid has been waiting, waiting to have you touch her emaciated limbs, and breathe upon her pallid brow. She has talked of your gentle eyes

and tender smiles, throughout the dreary months
when the storm-blast darkened the iron heavens,
and the north-wind shook the couch where she lay.
Yet she was not entirely bereft of comfort. Thanks
to you, and the good heavens! she saw you in her
dreams. In her sleep she often felt your soft hand
leading her along the sunny valleys, and heard the
blackbirds singing among the alders. How great
must be your beauty, lovely Spring, since she thus
beheld you in her dreams, and smiled as an infant
to meet its absent mother. Her eyes, too, lighted
up, though faintly, when they rested on some pot-
ted flowers, which at your last visit you kindly left
her; and she made me promise to take care of and
cherish the poor dear things when she herself should
be no more. Ardently she longed once more to
behold her much-loved Spring; but, alas, she died
without the blessed sight. And now you will not
leave us, will you, without sprinkling her lonely
grave with those beautiful violets she so much liked
and resembled.

One other person hails your benignant advent with
a youthful, childish delight. It is she who has lis-
tened to the tempests of nearly ninety winters, and
cannot " stand against their awful cold." She has
been watching and watching for your white velvet
clouds, that she may feast her dim eyes again upon
their dusky skirts, and enjoy the light and heat re-

flected from their round shining borders. The spirit of the aged turns with the flowers towards the sun, as a friend old enough to remember them in days that are gone, and shudders at the approach of winter, wailing with its sobbing winds over long mournful shadows, the legacy of departed summer, and frightful frosts sealing up the warm currents of animal and vegetable life. Though ready for departure, Nature yet shrinks with dismay from taking it at that pitiless season amid the strife of the elements, and seeking its dreary home beneath the bleak, ice-ribbed clod. Tremblingly therefore does the poor nonagenarian look out of the window in the season of snows, and fervently invoke the visit of the sweet south-winds which usher in the Spring, those "sightless couriers of the air," that come dropping tears along their journey from the tropics, over regions of slavery and wrong.

Now the lambent fires of Sirius, and the golden orbs of Orion, marshalled onward by the Hyades, and Venus, most beautiful of all, are shining in the soft evening sky, and rural sounds begin to be heard in the plains. Quickly does her eager ear catch the pipings of the frogs in the lagunes, — a solitary, timid note at first, but soon swelling out into a lusty Hallelujah chorus. What mellow thoughts of other years revive with the simple melody of the harbinger Spring-Bird perched upon the picket in the fence! The redbreast whistles in the apple-tree, or runs along the ground, stopping now and then to perk up his head and take an observation. The bluebird warbles among the garden shrubbery just bursting into life, and the heart of the aged expands under the all-dissolving reign of Spring.

All sigh and watch for the young coquettish Spring, except the prisoner in his solitary cell. The pleasant revolution of the seasons is a blank to him. The murmur of the running brooks he cannot hear, nor see the brisk little tadpoles, overflowing with the ecstasy of new life just infused into them by a vernal sun; sculling with their one oar about the warm muddy pools by the road-side. The time for the singing of birds is come, but not to him, as the months and years roll by his dungeon, unmeasured by the shadow on the dial, or the sands dropping in the hour-glass.

> "Seasons return; but not to him returns
> Day, or the sweet approach of ev'n or morn,
> Or sight of vernal bloom, or summer's rose,
> Or flocks, or herds, or face divine of friend:
> But cloud instead, and ever-during dark
> Surrounds him, from the cheerful ways of men
> Cut off, and for the book of knowledge fair
> Presented with an universal blank
> Of nature's works, to him expunged and ras'd."

But the freeman, the denizen of the glorious unmanacled air, leaps with rapture on the approach of

Spring. And why should he not? Is it nothing that Nature then has a resurrection, and comes forth from the grave? Reviving animation returns to her shrunken features like health diffusing itself slowly over the pale face of a convalescent. Innumerable black or shining insects are creeping forth along the sand, or among the starting grass, while birds in flocks, or each severally on his own account, are "making a note of them," and seriously meditating on taking some individuals home for dinner. Luxurious repasts have the bright birds in the merry Spring-time, and famous appetites for sauce after their long winter Ramadan! But moderation is a maxim, in their feasts of reason and flow of song, and they leave intemperance to man.

As the farmer breaks up the steaming earth with his plough, the chivalrous cock, quitting his winter-quarters with his numerous household, follows along the dark, fat furrows, and helps himself and them to the richest vermicelli, — only for the stooping. What crops are theirs! The cottager may bless his stars, if his own shall be as good. Does not the good-natured, matronly cow, think you, now enjoy the yellow sunshine in the barn-yard? Undoubtedly she does, if there is any truth in physiognomy. How sleepy is her large, soft, dark-blue eye, as she gently chews her quiet cud, — not of tobacco, mind you, but comfort and reflection! What can she possibly be dreaming of, I wonder? I cannot tell. Perhaps of the new pasture, where she has spent the day, with its nice clear spring. Perhaps of — nothing at all; that is, I fancy, the happiest state — for a poor beast.

The Spring, like a true and lovely woman, as she is, (though the ancients, I believe, did not decide upon her gender,) is mightily pleased with her new dress, and cannot refrain from joyously dancing in the branches of the budding trees, and along the trembling vines. In her exuberant gayety she summons to her festival all the tribes of animated beings to behold her, and minister their praise. But I will not charge her with being vain. No, indeed. It cannot be vanity — can it? — to be conscious of one's real charms; and who shall deny to the possessor of beauty the pleasure of admiring, a very little, what makes the highest happiness of all others? It is a hard case, truly, when one is not permitted to enjoy one's own property.

And now, sweet Spring, tarry with us as long as possible; for we shall too soon bitterly regret your absence, after you are gone; and, alas! I know not if I may ever see you more.

ODE.

As once, upon a summer's day,
I on a bed of roses lay,
It chanc'd that Cupid sought the bow'r,
To point his dart, and sleep an hour.

Said I, " Who fears your little arrow?
I 'm sure, it cannot hurt a sparrow.
Though you may sting me, like the bee,
You must again, as well as he,
Extract the barbèd dart away,
Or harmless be another day."

With roguish look, and lip of pride,
The Paphian Boy, displeased, replied:
" Though time may cure the shallow smart
Inflicted by the insect-dart;
Though, if he let the sting remain,
He never more can hurt again:
You well shall know, before we part,
What 't is for Love to wound the heart, —
How harmless every dart must be,
Compar'd with th' arrow shot by me."

He, rising, waves his spangled wings,
And round him heavenly fragrance flings;
Loud rings his bow, his arrows fly:
" Oh, cruel Love, I die, I die.
The fiery shafts of heav'n above
Must yield to those of conquering Love."

SPARE THAT BIRD.

DON'T fire at that little bird, my good fellow. He has never done you any harm ; neither defrauded you of your property, attacked your person, nor spoken a word against your character. Why do you wish to take his life, which some among mankind believe is never forfeited for offences even of the darkest dye? What! you say, he is a thief. This is a matter to be proved; we are not willing to take the wolf's word against the lamb. " He steals the cherries; he scratches up the peas ; he robs us of the corn." These are indeed sharp accusations against a co-inheritor of the free air and the common, unlimited champaign. The bird has never recognized your monopolizing doctrines. He supports the bill that supports him — the land-limitation bill; and if the first discoverer of territory has superior claims, he puts in for being lord paramount of the greater part of the earth, and the sum total of the skies.

He is a thief, forsooth! because he takes a bite of a cherry, and helps himself and little ones occasionally to a dinner of sweet herbs eaten with a loving heart, or a dessert of over-ripe fruit, which might have rotted and been lost, had he not stept in to save it. And for this, and such as this, must the delinquent die and his whole race with him, just as if they were no better than so many buffaloes or Indians? There is no justice at all in this. Is not the bird at once a tenant in common of the farm, and an active partner in the cultivation of the fruit and grain? Everybody knows this is the truth. He diligently labors in the morning long before his human confederate is up, and while the owner of the soil in fact is little better than a sleeping partner. For hours he clambers about the trees, picking up a grub here, the egg of a canker-worm there, sometimes attacking the caterpillar in his den, sometimes cutting off destroying insects, while actually on a foraging party or marauding expedition at the very outposts of the branches. By all this perpetual watchfulness and ceaseless industry he and the farmer secure a bountiful and luscious crop. Shall he be denied a share of the proceeds? Shall he not bring in his bill for his wages? We tell you that whatever the courts below may do about the matter, the chancery of the skies will award him his righteous dues. These creatures of the Good Being shall be fed from the finest of the grain which they have watched over, and protected from the devouring enemy, while man has been asleep, or else too purblind to have guarded it himself, had he been ever so wide awake.

We take a pride in saying that many legislatures have seen this matter in its proper light, and vindicated the character of their own race by protecting that of our feathered friends. It is no more than right ; for the inhumanity of man to man takes a fearful lesson from inhumanity to bird and beast. It is no more than necessary. Ah ! my good fellow, you may say what you please about your shooting the little bird for the injury he does, or for the food which his delicate flesh affords. We know better. You kill him, because you love to do it. You have a despot's heart beneath your ribs ; and so have most other boys who like to hurt and wound, to tyrannize and destroy.

There is much unreflecting cruelty in the world, which injures, not from bad intention, but from the want of any mind at all. The butcher is the cause of infinite, needless agony in the exercise of his necessary and respectable vocation, from mere want of thought ; and habit has closed the hearts of thousands to practices of great barbarity. But with cases such as these, we have nothing now to do. We wish to deal with the scores of hard-hearted boys who impose on the loving nature of their dogs, and habitually treat them harshly. They take pleasure in teaching them knowing tricks, each of which they imprint indelibly on the poor dumb beast by painful stripes. We want to rap the knuckles of hundreds who love to tear the limbs of insects and small animals, not for the love of science, but that of witnessing their sufferings. We want to rebuke the wretches who stun frogs with stones to see them quiver, put butterflies on the rack to admire their colors, and maim the fly and beetle to find out what extremity of pain they can endure and live.

We should despair of bringing up a boy to be careful of the feelings of a man, if he spent his youth in the indulgence of wanton cruelty to his dog that shares his dinner; the insect crawling in his path; the horse, the profitable slave of man; the patient ox; and especially the gladsome choristers of the fields. In gratifying your appetite for torturing and killing, don't imagine for a moment, you persecutors of little birds, that you have any better apology to allege than the single one that you like to kill, because it is good sport. That is all. You shoot a singing-bird for the same reason that you pester and hector a boy that is weaker than yourself. It is an amusement. You know the bird is an innocent creature, a delightful ornament, a charm to the country, an inestimable accessory to man in protecting his property from the ravages of vermin, by which he more than earns his daily bread. Yet you persist in knocking him down, and robbing his nest, with no more remorse than if he were a viper or an oyster. We see how it is: you must have something to plague, and vex, and make uncomfortable. We recognize that feature in your nature, and now propose to cater for, and gratify it, on condition that you spare that bird and the tree among whose branches he discourses to us such beautiful music, all gratuitously. We hereby abandon to you — though not to torture, mind, but only murder — the various tribes of noxious insects, beasts, and birds of prey. You shall have the sea-serpent and the rhinoceros to sport with. Do what you please, so that you do it quickly, with the rattlesnake and skunk. The squash-bug, the caterpillar, and canker-worm shall be yours to crush between your thumb and finger; and we will even find no fault if you exterminate the moth, the bed-bug, cockroach, and mosquito. If a range like this has not room and verge enough for your diversion, when you grow up, we may perhaps give you the enemies of your country to hunt and shoot at; but, at present, we beseech you, spare that sweet little singing-bird now warbling in the tree-top; for he has a mate not far away, and a family of little ones in a nest close by; and he is expected every moment to return to them, and drop a crumb of something into their waiting mouths wide open to receive it.

INFLUENCE OF PLACE ON CHARACTER.

ID you ever notice, in the course of your travels, how people change in coming from the country to the city only in the course of a single day? It was more observable in the times when stage-coaches were the vehicles for travellers than now. Starting on a beautiful serene morning from the quiet, cosy, country village, where it had been calling round from house to house for passengers, every inmate of the coach felt introduced to one another by the simple circumstance of such accidental position ; or from belonging to the same vicinity, or town, at least for the time. On these easy and companionable terms they jogged along from town to town, occasionally taking in a passenger, and then again letting one out ; but still keeping the number good as the principal ones continued in company, for they were going to the great city.

But when they arrived within a dozen miles or so of the metropolis, a new face began gradually to creep over the company, or rather a new expression over their faces. Till then, no difference was per-

ceptible between the city and the country-bred.
All were equal and sympathetic. Now they silently lay aside by degrees their sweet, natural
companionship, and resume the old conventional
badges of distinction, which had been forgotten
among the mountains. The hard and disagreeable
characteristics of social castes begin to darken ; and
the late chatting, charming party, which set out
together in the morning, and made each other
happy throughout the day, has dissolved and disappeared like the morning dew, and other very different actors have taken their places. It is a shocking metamorphosis to those who experience it for
the first time. But it is so common to many now,
such as visitors to watering-places and the like, that
they soon cease to mind it. The effect which *place*
has on persons brings to mind a homely comparison ; and as it really resembles the operation that
rennet has on milk, souring, and resolving it into
substances of very unlike qualities and appearance,
we see no reason why the likeness, though vulgar,
shall not be noticed.

This deterioration of character in persons approaching the city from rural scenes of more equal
and sociable intercourse has in some respects a parallel in the mountain stream. Issuing from lofty
recesses, the water at first is delightfully soft and
pure. Soon it becomes a river from little tributary

accretions along its banks, continuing to be marked by the same qualities, till it nears the ocean. Then it gradually acquires the impurities of a dense population, and the hard brackish character of the mighty reservoir of waters, and at last mingles with its waves, and loses its sweetness and softness forever.

4

TÒ ΚΑΛÒΝ — THE BEAUTIFUL.

O Love! O ever-gushing fountain!
  I see thee in the radiant bow;
The champaign, cataract, and mountain
  In thy celestial essence glow.
Spirit of Beauty! thou hast given
Their lustre to the earth and heaven.
  Without thy subtle power,
The breathing canvas, statue, frieze,
Instinct with elements to please,
  Would please no more.

Yet, not for this, would I adore thee;—
  The viewless realm of mind is thine;
The good, the beautiful in story,
  In patriot, martyr, glorious shine.
Eternal, amaranthine splendors
Surround their country's true defenders;
  The faithful and the just,
Shall bourgeon in perpetual youth
When everything is dead but truth,
  And turned to dust.

In woman both of these are blending, —
  The matchless shape, the seraph soul;
With sweetest harmony contending
  To make a lovely, perfect whole.
A double beauty thus combining,
Woman and angel intertwining,
  Earth-born, yet from above;
'T is here THE BEAUTIFUL we find,
The fair in form, the pure in mind,
  Commanding love.

THE LOOKER-ON.

THE love of standing still and seeing other people work is developed early. It is at first apparently as insignificant as it is simple; but, like all the laws of Nature, turns out, on nice investigation, to be the cause of much of what we do, as well as a large proportion of all we suffer. To climb into a position where one can overlook the labors of his fellow-creatures, toiling and sweating along life's thoroughfares, while he is himself far above the dust of the crowd, is one of the strong motive-powers for striving to be rich. For to be rich without poor people to look down upon, would not give anybody pleasure. How many would be content to ride imprisoned in a pine box pulled along by horses on a laughing day in Spring, instead of bathing all over in the open air, and feeling the exquisite thrill of locomotion in the sweet sunshine, were there no pedestrians to compare themselves with, as they rolled along? A child is the best philosopher in this department of natural science; let him answer. This principle is pleasure-giving, but not productive; fitting one to receive impressions, not to make them. And it is remarkable that all of us have five organs for the former, to one only for the latter office. If some shall choose to contend that the tongue is an overmatch for all the five senses put together, we will not stop now to debate the point.

We have sometimes thought that to this source was to be attributed the delight of gazing on the moving of the silver-edged billowy cloud, the rolling sea, the dashing cataract. All these are ministers of exquisite enjoyment to the spectator, as at his leisure he overlooks Nature thus at her work. These and other objects of a similar kind do not consequently please equally well in painting; for the process of labor is not visible there. Instead of her actual operations, there is indeed the work of the artist, but it is already done. We prefer to see Nature, or somebody as her substitute, actually at her easel of creation. Many go to view a mountain, or a river now; but what a concourse would be present on notice given that either of them on a certain hour was to be thrown up, or poured down, before us, on the level prairie, or rocky ravine!

That the early Spring possesses a charm superior to all other seasons of the year is owing probably to some such metaphysics as that we have alluded to. Man is admitted then to Nature's workshop.

The world is not indeed about to be created absolutely out of nothing. That grand drama in six acts undoubtedly is over, though some philosophers in Massachusetts, we believe, are of opinion it is yet performing. But even these adepts will probably admit that the process is kept secret from all but very scientific eyes. To the common mass of us in this quarter, creation may be deemed as perfectly finished, unless we are ourselves able to catch Nature at some odd time in the actual manufacture of a fern, or fish. But to this drama of creation there is added every year a kind of after-piece of not quite so original but still delightful materials — the *renovation* of the natural world. At the moment we are writing, for example, one has only to look abroad in order to behold the most wonderful of spectacles, the miracle of the year, the resurrection of Nature from her annual sleep. The snow-drop, crocus, hyacinth, or some yet more tiny plant, wakes first, and utters a trill so soft and high as to be inaudible to mortal sense. But by and by the willow, the oak, and the whole vegetable kingdom arouse, and, aided by myriads of insect and animal voices, begin a chorus which is soon to run in successive fugues along the parallels from the Equator to the Pole.

Here is a real feast for man. He takes his seat in the boxes or parquet of this great natural amphitheatre, overhears all, overlooks all, *and does nothing.* One tree is bursting its buds, another is getting into flower as fast as possible; every blade of grass is growing green and growing tall with all its might, both day and night,—for Nature, after so long a nap, now, like Macbeth, sleeps no more,—every little creature that has a voice is practising and rehearsing to be ready for the universal oratorio or opera, which is soon to burst upon the ears of the universe, whether they have tickets or not, in gratuitous profusion, without regard to position, property, or power;—those indeed who have the least of these, and such as these, will probably get most music.

While the whole wide-spread creation is in this paroxysm of labor, we have forgotten man, the lord of all. He of course is the master of the ceremonies, the leader, the conductor of the whole. If *we* have forgotten that gentleman, he has by no means forgotten himself on this occasion, any more than on others. He rubs his hands; he rubs his eyes; the sight evidently affects him. But he does not lead the orchestra of jubilant thanksgiving. He has a previous engagement in Tripler Hall, the Opera House, or the World's Fair. He never sings except to tickets. The Nightingale — (the real, not the mock-bird, we mean) — may perform gratuitously, if she pleases; but not he. And what *does* he do to celebrate this resurrection of a world?

Nothing. The lazy creature loves to feel, accept, receive, to be obliged. It is his happiness to oversee; so he watches the young apples and peaches growing. He admires to see them turning red, and when they are tired of ripening and fall to the ground, he picks them up and eats them. He rejoices also to see the sheep and oxen as they labor, and particularly as they are grazing in the rich pastures and waxing fat. He exerts himself so far even as to make a particular noise with his lips when he anticipates the time that they shall pay for their *good living* by becoming so to him.

Next to the pleasure of overlooking people when they are actually at work, is that of examining their work after it is executed. The charm of the London Fair probably consists in this. It will be much less than the enjoyment which the curious looker-on would have had in watching the various processes which brought about such astonishing results of art, as some of them will doubtless be; but it is better than nothing. The spectator may put his hands within his pockets, while he is gazing at the contents of the Crystal Palace, and imagine he is looking on a host of black-faced, tough-handed mechanics, hammering, punching, shaving, and blowing and straining to his utmost satisfaction. It is the truth; his fancy has not deceived him, and he has a right to enjoy the picture.

This principle of our excellent human nature accounts, as we suppose, for the legion of commentators every day increasing, that are found sticking, like aphides on a rose-bush, to the works of famous men, of Shakspeare, Goethe, Raphael, and the rest. With such a load of barnacles adhering to their bottoms, we should once have feared that with such men as we have mentioned, the Homers, Virgils, and Phidiases of antiquity would never have been able to sail down the stream of time to the present generation. But experience has proved the contrary, and we believe now, notwithstanding the comments and praises of the critics, that the works of these celebrated persons will float some time longer yet. In the mean time, the myriads of industrious, painstaking scholiasts, who have feasted on the choice fruits of other men's brains, have felt a happiness for which they doubtless were peculiarly organized. Some animals are formed to feed on one another, and some on substances not quite so distinctly appropriated. Notwithstanding such unfavorable appearances, they are doubtless both equally well employed in their different vocations.

We would not for a moment call in question the right of any one to admire to the utmost superlative of extravagance the works of his favorite author, painter, or musician. But we have sometimes wished, we must acknowledge, that he had kept a portion of it to himself.   When such an individual finds he is accumulating a critical stock beyond the demand of his own consumption, of course he favors the public with the balance; there seems to be no help for it.   The strength of the propensity to be nothing but a witness in the perpetual trials of life, or, what is much the same, of feeding upon others' earnings, will forever render the spectator tribe out of all proportion to the productive, as horse-flies must always be more numerous than horses.   Some of the speculations of these parasitical observers are like green fruit, neither fit for one's own use, nor the market.   Such are the disquisitions of certain persons upon Art.   According to their theory, a man is nothing but a laborer or mechanic when he executes a beneficial work; to be an artist, he must be useless.   Art, like the Egyptian emblem of eternity, — the extremity-joined circular serpent, — ends in itself, and has no other end, or aim, or purpose.   It teaches nothing, aspires to nothing, above or beyond itself, and worships nothing but the ideal, now corrupted to mean idol. A moral intention debases the picture or the statue, as a work of art, and nothing of truth is tolerated but its nakedness; its principle being inconsistent with high excellence.   He who performs a work for a livelihood or pay is a laborer or mechanic; to be a gentleman he must live without work, or work without reward.

These sentiments, though bad enough, and shocking to the right-principled soul, are not more disgusting to the taste than the cool pretension of that growing class who periodically gabble about music. Beethoven and the Germans are their peculiar province; yet they exercise a jurisdiction over the whole domain of the art. If they are to be credited, music is a universal language, expressing ideas, as well as emotions. They can clearly see what the composers could not do themselves, — a drama in an overture of Mozart, and an epic poem in a symphony of Beethoven. Even the initiated differ very materially in their translations from the score, and to everybody else the whole is little better than heathen Greek.

The man who plays the part of spectator, or auditor, through life, contracts a comfortable opinion of his own capacity and powers. Did anybody ever observe a potter moulding with his hands the rotating clay into an earthen jug? The looker-on thinks it very easy, and is certain he can do the same. A trial would undeceive him, and destroy his vanity; of that, however, our friend is in no danger; so he continues to look, and to look, to the end of his pilgrimage, congratulating himself abundantly all the while upon his power to paint, and preach, and write, as others do, if he should only make the attempt. Poor man! he sometimes fancies he plays the game which he only overlooks, and if he ever has the luck to detect a false move, a defective measure, or an imperfection in a drawing, it is a capital for him to put on interest for the remainder of his life. The world hears it forever to his last day, and to our fortunate critic the recollection of it always comes with all the freshness of the first achievement.

THE SONNET.

Is aught on earth so beautiful to see
   As a young mother and her rosy child?
She fondles it, she trots it on her knee,
   And almost smothers it with kisses wild.
Oh, yes! It is that mother when she smiled
   At some sweet thought that none had thought before;
   Some child of genius, which her fancy bore
To show conflicting beauties reconciled.
   She sits, caressing o'er and o'er again
   This tender offspring of her teeming brain;
The baby-stranger with the daintiest taste
   She dresses, teaches him to warble, yet
In fettered numbers exquisitely graced,
   So makes her *son* at last a rare *sonnet*.

NOVEMBER.

A SONNET.

NOVEMBER! last of mellow Autumn's train,
  The world, enervate with the balmy air
  And soft caresses of thy sisters fair,
Call thine a gloomy, melancholy reign.
  But come, ye sland'rers, to the sunny plain,
And see the butterfly o'er fern and flower
  Pursue his yellow mate with effort vain,
While th' Indian Summer pours a golden show'r.
  But ah! the vision changes as I write!
The ragged clouds in black procession rise,
  They quench the hazy sun in sudden night,
And Winter sternly rules the iron skies.
  Thou canst, like man, assume a pleasant face,
  In both 't is often nothing but grimace.

THE WAY TO ENJOY THE COUNTRY.

HOW much are those mistaken creatures to be pitied, who suppose the country is, or ought to be, just like the city, only having a purer and cooler air. In the last they are miserably disappointed ; and, if the heat were all that makes the crowded town uncomfortable in the dog-days, going into the country would be a miserable blunder.

But the breezes are purer; granted. And is that all ? By no means. Yet it is all to many, perhaps a majority of citizens. It is all the change they wish or feel. Everything beside must be precisely like the city, — dress, style of living, parlor-manners, etiquettes, and employment of time. Truly, the change of earth and skies avails but little, if the old routine is to be preserved. But a change of habits and tastes will be found upon experiment to be much more difficult, as well as important, than any and every other. Horses, steamboats, and cars can in a few hours bring about the one ; the other will take time and a course of lessons, and then perhaps fail of success.

For just consider the contrast between the city and the country, — one so full of excitement, the other so placid and quiet. One absolutely forces occupation and amusement upon you, the other leaves you to yourself; you must make your own entertainment, or go without it. To extract — we do not say the peculiar pleasures of rural life — but any pleasure at all, one is to wander about, not upon flag-stones, but over fields of bushes or grass, now scratched by the thorn, or entangled in the meshes of the blackberry-vine; sometimes feeling the cool water of deceptive places in the meadow gently running over the tops of his shoes. In the country, we lie lazily, dreamily, under the darting and dodging lights and shadows of a big chestnut-tree, not reading poetry, like a sickly sentimentalist in town, but listening to the poet's original inspirers, — the cat-bird singing in the thicket, the thrush upon the maple, trying to rival the mocking-bird, not without some success. Hear the honest robin — a bit of a thief we confess, when cherries are ripe — warbling his cheerful song, or startling one with his loud note of surprise or alarm.

But if any of you have a taste for articulate music, measured by graceful motion, you will never cease to take delight in the company of the plump black and white bobolink, whose rich notes gush out at the moment of his taking wing. We see him now (in the mind's eye) hovering over the sweet red clover with his curved bat-like wings, singing all the while he is gradually descending to light upon the top of the fragile spire of grass, which, of course, sinks beneath his weight, and lets him down to the ground, where he finds his lady; if not, why then some lady-*bug*, which will do as well, his appetite being prepared for either fortune.

But it is not all half-shut-eyed indolence in the country, reposing beneath mighty oaks and chestnuts, watching the motions of their great outspread arms, and listening to the whistling of the winds that causes them. It is delicious, we grant, to hear these, and see the dancing lights and shades around, and the fleets of sailing clouds above, bearing all sorts of pennons, while the mower is swinging his scythe in the meadow below, or on the hill-side opposite, with as much grace and rhythm as Jullien does his *bâton.* Ah! there is music in harmonious labor, as well as in the operas (*works*) of Rossini! There is utility too in both, though one is immediately productive, the other not. We acknowledge it here in the midst of the ploughmen and cultivators, sons of the sickle and the scythe.

Rural enjoyments are not all thus somnolent, passive, and sensuous. Do you hear that brook, now quiet, now brawling? It is denominated a trout-stream, and the noise heard is said to be a conversation between that shy creature and his neighbor, the Naiad. You have seen the elegant fishing-tackle, which nothing that has fins, it would seem, could ever escape? Well, that is made for this very rivulet. It was invented for this very trout-brook. Now throw it in, and troll and travel, troll and travel, hour after hour. Have you caught anything in all that weary tramp? " Why, no, nothing but happiness and health ; I have been expecting every minute to lay the glittering prize upon the green bank, but have not had a bite as yet — perhaps I shall."

It has frequently been mooted, whether fishing for amusement is right — is it Christian ? There is no difficulty in replying. It is perfectly moral, in our opinion, for every city-gentleman to buy fishing-tackle of great price and murderous look, and use it also with all his skill, in as many trout-streams as he pleases. From our own experience in such matters we are willing to say, " the blood of all the trout, which they may catch, be upon us and on our children ! " We will be responsible for all the misery they will cause the fish. But, though the pretty tenants of the water may be missed, the mark the sportsman aimed at has been hit. He may carry home no exquisitely sweet trout for breakfast, yet he will thus have a keener relish for his codfish-balls and mutton-chop.

The piscatory game, at which, as in most others, very little is to be won but by adepts, yields nothing directly to the player, at least nothing he expected, but a great deal that he did not; this pastime is not the only one in the power of visitants from the town. There is fowling, facetiously called sporting, — *lucus a non lucendo,* — sporting, because there is not a bit of fun in it. Here the question again arises, Is it morally lawful to kill birds? First, be our choicest anathemas on all destroyers of singing-birds. Secondly, on all others of the feathered tribe not intended for consumption. We have a right to live on them, if we can catch them, because they themselves subsist on all the insects they can get. But the point is quite a useless one to make, so far as concerns our city-gentlemen who purchase their first-rate fowling-pieces of the crack vender. Friends! you need not be so particular about your powder. Take our word for it, almost any sort will answer. Twenty to one, you will never have a chance to burn it unless in blazing away at a swallow, which is villainous, or a tom-cat, which is patriotic, — no, not even at a sham representation of Princeton battle.

Only reflect what a sportsman has to go through. Through rivers up to his hat in water, — through swamps over his boots in mud, — creeping on his belly without either hat or boots, pushing his gun

before him, — all this, too, for a single bird weighing four ounces, and half that when drest! Is it
not delightful? Do you suppose now, that a city-
gentleman with white pants glistening with the recent iron, Parisian boots and gloves, indescribable
coat, waistcoat, and nethers, is going through this
purgatory to fit him for the joys of participating in
the paradise of a dish of woodcock and snipe,
weighing two ounces with their insides, all told?
No, no! he will do all that may become a man, —
gentleman, we mean, — anything more is nought.

So far as these citizens are concerned, no harm to
the beautiful people need be apprehended; their
lives may be insured for a small premium at any of
the offices. But for those whelps who go about
shooting-sparrows, wrens, and such like, together
with singing-birds, — creatures who would willingly
associate, assist, and please man, if not driven away
by fraud and violence, — we heartily wish, when
they go upon such expeditions, that they may jointly
and severally carry with them a gun of that kind
spoken of by " Hudibras," which kicked its owner
over.

PARALLEL BETWEEN A MOSQUITO AND A FLY.

 FLY is a small insect, but a mosquito is much smaller. The former has a short bill, the latter one almost equal to that of a woodcock. When we consider the use each makes of this weapon of his, or, more properly, tool for getting a living with, the diversity is still more marked, for the fly labors and procures his livelihood in the daytime; and when night comes on, however hungry he may be and keen his appetite, he calmly goes to rest with his tail uppermost, when his stomach is empty, just as we turn a tumbler upside-down when there is nothing in it. Or he may assume this posture in order that the humors of the body may settle into the head and produce a kind of lethargy and repose, as we take spirits that they may ascend into our brains and make them comfortable. The fly is more nimble in attack, and so marches up boldly in the daytime; while the mosquito, not so secure of effecting a safe retreat, takes

care to assault under cover of darkness. But we are far from inferring, therefore, that the former possesses a greater degree of courage. We don't believe that either of them have the folly of men to venture where they know that certain death awaits them.

Some have argued that the mosquito is the braver of the two, because he generously gives premonitory notice by his music. We believe in this chivalry of his just as much as we do in the rattlesnake who shakes his tail before a spring, to give fair warning, or in the gallantry of a burglar, who makes a noise in breaking through a window. The fact is, neither of them can help it. They would conceal their designs by approaching silently, like a cat, if they were able. But, fortunately, Nature has invented what we call noise, for the general safety, though it turns out to be rather annoying in particular cases. Thus Nature in this instance, as in thousands of others, is very conservative, and careful for the comfort and preservation of her creatures.

As in the case of princes, the reign of the personages we are comparing is of divers lengths of duration. In this the fly has a manifest advantage. It begins earlier and continues later. He has, beside, the advantage, as Dr. Franklin discovered, of an exemption from death by drowning; for, on being dried after a thorough water-soaking, he starts up as brisk as ever. We say nothing of their relative happiness on that account: there are insects whose lives are conjectured not to last beyond an hour, and even less. And yet it may be imagined they are as happy as they can be. If one's capacity for enjoyment is quite satisfied, he is full. What would you have more? The trouble with mankind is, their capacity for felicity is so very large that it takes an immense amount of happiness to fill it; the consequence is that few get anything like as much as they can hold, and want.

For these considerations, we will not distress ourselves about the happiness of flies and mosquitoes. They do very well, we dare say, in that respect; quite as well as some of those whose juices they are enjoying. There is a marked difference, however, in the reputation of the two. Flies, though much more numerous in our dwellings, are nevertheless much less unpopular, and treated with far more lenity. What Uncle Toby ever took a mosquito between his thumb and finger, and let him go with a whole skin again? Not only so, but, more especially, what good-natured fellow ever made a speech to him on performing such a benevolent act, in the words of that gentleman, which we do not literally remember, but were to this effect, as he tossed him gently out of the window, " Go, poor wretch; the world is wide enough for thee and me."

This difference in public estimation is no doubt
due to the different style of their housekeeping.
The fly lives on almost everything upon the table,
or off it. He dives into this pot and cup and
that, and buries himself in sugar or molasses. We
only brush him away; that's all. He is feeding
just like ourselves, and loves the same things. But
the mosquito is a carnivorous bird of prey; he
scents blood, and *our* blood too, in particular. If
he would sit down to table with us, as the genial
fly does, and partake of things there as they are going, like a gentleman, he might enjoy himself up to
the eyes, with now and then a gentle remonstrance,
if he should bring too many friends to dine with
him. But he is not satisfied with this. The Shy-
lock demands our flesh and blood for his gratification, and is not content with what is set before him.
Flesh and blood won't bear this. This is his offence; and for this truculent and sanguinary temper
and practice capital punishment is awarded him;
and all proclaim it just.

Men are not their only enemies. The spider
spreads his net to ensnare them; but though he
seems to do very little else than wait for them, and
other small game, he does not on the whole, as it
appears, do a very large business in catching flies or
mosquitoes. The latter are indeed a dry morsel
enough, and unless recently gorged with blood, must

be hardly worth the notice and picking of so intelligent a creature as the spider; for a mosquito is little better than a skeleton, or sculpin. On the other hand, a fly is a portly fellow, and offers more tempting refreshment to the fasting gentleman in black, who lives not to work, but to eat and grow fat. After all, though the natural enemy of the two, the spider does the race very little harm. It is the frost that

> "Cuts down all,
> Both great and small,"

among the insect tribes.

On the whole, we consider the mosquito the highest and fastest liver; but, as often happens in such cases, not the happiest individual. He suffers from intemperance. Their genius is about alike; but, as to habits, the fly is to be preferred for his more social disposition, and his early retirement to bed, while his rival is cruising about o' nights in bed-chambers and elsewhere. As to personal appearance, the fly has the advantage, being plump and comely, whereas the mosquito is gaunt, and has a hungry, hawkish, sinister look. The latter excels in voice, the other in quickness of parts. One sees best in the daytime, the other in the night. The fly is a fine convivial companion at all our meals, and sticks to one sometimes like a burr, or a dog. In their sense of smell also, which is remarkable, they both resemble that animal not a little.

BABIES.

BABY has fallen down stairs. Very natural. Of course every baby falls down stairs once. That is not the worst of it. As it grows up, it does most of the other tricks its parents did when they were young, notwithstanding all their wise saws now to the contrary. Can you convince a boy that a cigar is a nasty weed, or wine and brandy poisons, till he has tried and found them so, as you did? What is the use of preaching to Miss not to pinch her waist or appetite, till she has found out by ill health the folly of the practice, and that it is a real suicide.

Baby must have its dolls and drums and trumpets; and, when grown older, will insist on more of the same sort of toys, though at a more extravagant cost. Can you prevent it? See if you can prevent baby's tumbling down stairs, or bumping its head against the table, or bruising its nose sometimes, or getting into hot water at other times! You cannot do it. Your grandfather and grandmother both did the same, and so did you. What is to be done then?

Experience must be bought with a price, no less than that of bloody noses and black and blue spots. It is the law of expansion and growth. The experience of another is naught. Each for himself must try all things, and hold fast that which is good. You might as well expect to thrive by getting another to eat your dinner for you, as to hire him to go through experiences for you. Baby grows taller through the several divisions of inches on Gunter's, just as you did; and also grows wiser by making the same experiments of life, of pleasure, and of pain.

Did you ever mind how the old trick of plucking forbidden fruit, learnt in the world's infancy, is universally prevalent with children now? They seem to love to put their little hands upon things on purpose to have you say, Ah! ah! ah! When they have, by pretending to seize something, forced from you a refusal, they are quite satisfied, for their object is attained. There is abundance of fun and humor in them. The spirit of adventure, romance, and drollery appears early. In fact, we very soon see in them the embryo of all they will be. They discover bravery by venturing to the verge, self-sufficiency by assuming the exclusive control of playthings, perseverance by insisting on what they have once made up their minds to have, and the like.

And yet the child is the slave of imitation. Take care, then, what temper and manners you exhibit in their presence; for, be assured that an orange is not more certain to impart its flavor to what is brought into contact with it than children are to take their character from associates. In this respect we perpetuate ourselves in our children, who may be said to resemble those modern towns which are built from the materials of ancient cities.

A PASSAGE OF LIFE.

At church, upon the Sabbath-day,
In the next pew but one,
A lady sat alone.
She neither serious seemed, nor gay;
I hope it was not wrong to turn my eyes that way.

Her modesty took no alarm,
As if a glance at her
Meant aught particular;
Her beautiful form sustained no harm,
More than a rose would do iu scattering round its balm.

Along the range of gardens near
I marked a feeble light,
That shone through all the night,
And went not out, till daylight clear
Its modest, trembling lustre caused to disappear.

Each night I watched that glimmering flame;
More constant than the stars,
That in their silver cars
Roll nightly round th' ethereal frame,
This little light, through all the hours, shone still the same.

One night I missed its timid beam;
The stars shone as before,
But to my gaze no more
Appeared that solitary gleam,
Which vanished like the baseless fabric of a dream.

An interval had passed. Again
I occupied the place
Where first that lovely face
Diffused delight without a stain;
But she was veiled in sorrow's black funereal train.

What anguish in that bosom lay!
What visions of her breast,
In radiant colors drest,
Before that taper passed away,
While I with careless speculation watched its ray!

NO SABBATH FOR THEM.

THE Holy Sabbath — the quiet Sabbath — day of repose and serene meditation to the tired body, to the weary soul! A benediction art thou to thousands who are grateful for thy sweet return and gracious gifts, and to thousands on thousands more who are not conscious of, or do not acknowledge, the irredeemable debt they owe thee! One day in seven, snatched from labor, anxiety, and racking cares! One day of contemplation, turned upward from earth to heaven, from the world of friends we are leaving, or who are leaving us, to that which is to be our home, to the friendships never to be dissolved any more forever. What a statute that would be, which enacted that every seventh day should be devoted to rest, sacred to calm reflection, to happy thoughts! It is beyond the power of human legislatures to pass so beneficent and sublime a law, — to inaugurate an observance prefiguring not the exceptional but the uniform state of the blessed hereafter, when time will be absorbed in one eternal Sabbath of the soul. Of

this we have but a poor foretaste now, adulterate
in kind and restricted in duration, but, such as it
is, its felicity is yet denied to millions of our race.

The PHYSICIAN knows no Sabbath. Sickness
will not wait for work-days. Only in the Sabbath
of the future world will there be no sickness, neither sighing nor weeping. The purest here are not
exempt from natural ills, from accident, calamity,
and death. The physician therefore, the select warrior of mankind against disease, stands sentry every
hour of the day, every day of the week alike, and
must be ready for defence whenever the enemy,
who is no respecter of times and persons, shall
come by day or in the silent watches of the night.
He must be ever in armor to go forth and do battle
with " the pestilence that walketh in darkness, and
the devastation that wasteth at noonday."

The MOTHER knows no Sabbath. Her infant
may sleep, but her own eyelids must not close, or
only as the Æolian harp smiles into rest to reawaken
instantly when the next plaintive breath of air
sweeps over its sensitive chords. All days must be
alike to her, — in work and watchful care. Only
in the hidden recesses of her pious heart can she
feel the deep satisfaction of the Seventh Day. The
distant church-bell may vibrate on her ear ; perhaps
her heart may catch some notes of a neighboring
organ, vocal with the Creator's praise. But not for

her, who most needs them, are the soothing consolations, the sweet inspirations of the Sabbath-day. She must sit solitary in her chamber, or overwhelmed with maternal solicitudes without number. At one time her infant demands what no other than she can give. At another, a young and wayward child, though it may possibly dispense with a mother's hand, yet what mother will withdraw it, whenever it promises to be of the smallest service? — Now a child is sick, then one is suffering from an accident, needs correction, or cannot be left with another. In short, a mother, like Nature herself, "works always," is never at rest. Children, sick or well, are her delight; they are also her frequent vexation. If she plays, ever, it is with her children. If these are the family satellites, domestic astronomy differs widely from the celestial in this, for in the astronomy of the household, parents, and the large or primary bodies in general, revolve around the secondaries, or children; and if there happens to be a babe in the house, he is the very centre of attraction — the *primum mobile* of the whole system.

What then must be a mother's life, how importunate and engrossing her indispensable obligations, to keep in repair and healthy motion so complex and delicate a machine as a family of young children? How a care-taking mother ever survives, we wonder much. Affection must be the great sanitary agent; there is no other to account for the phenomenon. Without this panacea she could not outlive her sleepless nights, her unceasing agitations, petty solicitudes, and consuming fears. All these and more are hers to endure, and this too with scarcely a holiday to recruit her jaded body, or even a Sabbath to reinspire her soul pressed down to earth by a heavy bond of sometimes great and sometimes small anxieties, but always unremitting, never ending, though constantly beginning.

EXAGGERATION IN CONVERSATION.

EXAGGERATION may be a vice in some other nations, for aught we know, but we are sure it is the besetting sin of our own. " The house was crammed to the ceiling," we hear it reported, when the vacant seats would hold as many more. " The procession consisted of ten thousand well - dressed, respectable people ; " yet when counted they were after all but nineteen hundred and fifty persons, all told, there, and most of them were shabby fellows enough, some indeed just out of the penitentiary. Many have the habit of using the little but significant words, " never," " always," and the like, with a perfect looseness. " Jack, you are the laziest fellow existing, and never do anything from morning to night," whereas he had that very day, when this sweeping assertion was made, been running on nine errands for the complainant to the milliner, grocer, and dry-goods store, beside tending the cradle two hours together, and answering the door-bell seven times, to tell callers that the lady had gone into the country, — that is, was busy up-stairs preparing a dress for some of the anniversaries. We overheard one individual charging another with making a thousand mistakes in a piece of writing, which did not, on investigation, contain more than five hundred words in all. Moreover, this man alleged that a certain newspaper, notoriously carefully printed, "was always full of mistakes, the very worst in this respect in the whole country." On being challenged to point them out, he did not find one, but protested that he could, give him time.

This hyperbole of speech runs into extravagance of conduct, but of this nothing will now be said. Concerning this disagreeable trick of speech, it is to be remarked that it defeats itself. One cannot be positive about the statements of a man who has superlatives perpetually on his tongue. Overcharged assertions are falsehoods, though they may not be lies for the want of a malicious intent. But they wholly deprive the person employing them of all credit in his statements. He commits the very common mistake of destroying the vigor of his language by the intense and overwrought phrases which he thought would give it strength. The impression made by such a person is therefore feeble, his expressions being received as sound and fury, signifying nothing. The way to affect by language is to speak the truth in simplicity, nothing exaggerating,

and setting down naught in a false light.   Renounce
this injurious habit, for it robs the language of its
strength.   When superlatives and intense expressions are made to do service on trivial occasions,
nothing will be left for use at times when all the
resources of the language will be required as vehicles for thoughts the most powerful, and emotions
the most profound.

There is a species of exaggeration so bold, ingenious, and extraordinary as to deserve the name of
wit.   " His horse was not a circumstance to my
Arthur in speed.   Arthur outstripped him at once,
and was as much faster as lightning is than a funeral."   This is a not very strong example that just
occurs to us.   It runs in the blood of certain families, and is a kind of efflorescence of imagination
not under judicious restraint.   The mischief is, that
many believe they can exhibit this sort of talent, as
others think they can pun, when they cannot.   The
conversation of such persons, consequently, rarely
rises higher than that of those pretenders to smart
talk, who interlard all they have to say, sometimes
compose the staple of it, with some current cant
phrases.   One of these has made a large part of
some peoples' talk for several years past ; it is the
phrase "you know."

A gentleman of this school addressed us the other
day somewhat as follows : " On my arrival at Wash-

ington, *you know*, I was sent for by the President, *you know*, who wanted to see me on a matter of importance. I did not suppose I should see Miss Lane, *you know*, but I was shown, *you know*, by express command of the President, into the drawing-room where she was. I found her as charming in conversation, *you know*, as she was fascinating in person," &c., &c. Now I did not know any of these things, and, what is more, I did not believe them; but such poor gabble as this prevails extensively. Gentlemen, and sometimes ladies too, must have some cant word to bring in frequently to fill up, round off the style, and help them with its oar to skull along. Those who have the habit of profane swearing make use of the windy sails of oaths for this purpose, of which it must be said they are only worse than the everlasting *you know* one hears in all companies.

MAN WITH A CANE.

THE true secret in the economy of life, as well as in that of nature, seems to be to dispense with all show and expense not necessary for utility. Numbers all around us surpass this reasonable limit, and instead of proportioning their outlay to the end to be obtained, their ambition would appear to be to make as great an exhibition of their resources as they can, while they don't mind in the least how contemptible and inadequate the results may be. If two wheels of a carriage are sufficient, why add more? Still, if four have advantages, it is prudent to have them. But some limit must be imposed, and so mankind have hence conceived the aphoristic comparison that any superfluous object of foolish desire is no more wanted than a fifth wheel to a coach. The same idea is sometimes expressed to a child, whose little pockets and hands are already entirely full of *goodies* upon Christmas-Day, and who yet cries for more : — " My child," the father exclaims, " you do not need it any more than a toad wants a tail."

This thought suggests another, namely, whether a toad *does* really feel the want of that prolongation, or does not? If not, then another query follows: of what possible utility a tail can be to a turkey? Was its usefulness the final cause of its existence, or was the turtle, or tortoise, endowed with it as an ornament, with which he was enriched simply because he had a convenient shell or house to put it in, as the toad has not? But our plan is not to pursue the investigation now, if we ever do, but this whole question of how much is required for ornament, how much for comfort, and why men have but two legs, and horses have four, with the collateral inquiries of why they have no more, and why they have so many, when reptiles have none at all, — these reflections, we say, have suggested an observation of the means by which one of the animals mentioned — man — has attempted to supply the denials of Nature by inventing a kind of third leg for his own particular use.

For our own part, we never could be persuaded to purchase a CANE, or third leg, unless the seller would agree to send it home. An umbrella is rather more of this sort of thing than we are willing to lug about, and a handle without the silk expansion looks too much like a fool's bauble. But this absurdity is not perceived in the present fashion of carrying sticks in the hand, as baboons are described doing in their native forests, and we are acquainted with one excellent gentleman in particular, who has an uncommon passion for a stick, and exhibits his idiosyncrasy daily, by never going abroad, or anywhere indeed, on any account, without his cane.

It is indeed a very pretty India joint, with a handle of ivory, to which is attached a death-doing looking dagger; but the stick, when this is properly enclosed, and everything is in the right place, is a smooth, polished, and innocent appearing toy. Some characters resemble this beautiful cane very much, when in repose and made up for show, yet, as well as the India joint within that shining outside, contain a tiger which is capable, when unchained, of being aroused to deeds of anger and revenge.

For no such intent, however, does this gentleman make it his perpetual companion. He thinks no ill of others, and does not suspect any wrong from them. His poniard is therefore, at best, but a dormant partner. It is the cane which is his friend, not its contents. With this he sits, and stands, he rides, and walks. He parts not from it in-doors nor out-doors, in the parlor nor the chamber. He breakfasts, dines, and sups in its company, and, it is said, sleeps with his hand upon the ivory. Is it a talisman? We suppose it must be, for he pressed it against his chin, his lips, his cheek, his forehead,

his nose, as if to absorb its hidden virtue at every
pore.

Look out for the gentleman with the slender cane.
None need to fear, least of all to shun him, for he is
courteous, a man of honor and position. But he is
rather queer, is n't he? For one, however, we have
a liking for oddities, provided they are innocent.
They smack of mystery, excite curiosity, and add
variety to life; and variety, the copy-book says, is
charming.

Consequently we have a fancy for old Dr. David
Potter, who used to preach with a cane in his hand
to mark the emphasis in his forcible way; while
Dr. John B. Smith could not go on in his sermon
without carrying occasionally a little bit of paper
to his short-sighted eyes, though it was entirely
blank.

"POOR RICHARD" DENOUNCED.

IT is wonderful and almost incredible what an extent of influence is exerted in his proper sphere by every individual and agency in Great Britain to promote the vital interest of the nation — the supply of all creation with their manufactures. Their trading and industrial classes are everlastingly holding forth the doctrine that England has a kind of natural right to supply all the universe with every useful and ornamental ware, and that it is everybody's duty to apply to her workshops for everything they want. It is a matter of course that they should preach this doctrine in foreign parts, as well as at home. They would but half perform their work if they should produce the manufactures without sending out with them the arguments whereby their exclusive title to make them for the nations should be defended.

But a belief in the creed runs in the blood of every native of the Island. It would be a sufficient evidence that a man was not an Englishman, if such was not his undoubting faith. It is taught in childhood, and in the schools, and is among the number perhaps of their innate ideas, if there are any such. The persuasion grows with them and overshadows their reason, and the peculiar notion, as peculiar as anything in South Carolina, is disseminated in pamphlets and periodicals, and reeks in the newspaper press. We have heard, but are not sure, that what is thus spread by lay-preachers in the highways and by-ways of society, is sometimes inculcated in sermons. We have been told that books on the mathematics have been written to promote the designs of a party. We know that metaphysics have been made to descend from their pure and mysterious heights of absolute intellectuality to serve interested ends, and historic tomes been written to pander to a faction. We are, therefore, less surprised than we might otherwise be, that the remotest and least liable to be suspected agencies of opinion have been resorted to for the sake of poisoning the public mind with false ideas in political economy. Quarterlies might be expected to be purchased for this purpose, and magazines. But one is reluctantly compelled to believe that graver works are but treacherously pursuing the vocation which has been assigned them by the predominant genius and interest of a whole country, when we find them soberly, and with apparent sincerity, laying down principles of moral truth, to serve the purposes of gain. Yet, be not deceived. One must not listen too implicitly to the gravest and most edifying ethical lectures. Our fathers went to the cornfield armed, and on their watch against the faithless Indians. Their descendants must now examine every magazine and book with a certain *imprimatur* upon it, lest an asp may lie concealed beneath its perfidious leaves.

On taking up " Blackwood " not long ago, we were amazed to discover an artful writer there in favor of British manufactures, going a little beyond most of his tribe, and invading the seminal principles of human conduct — the very sources of thought. This is beginning at the beginning. He is, however, sagacious in his plan; would he were equally right in the end at which he is aiming!

Would you believe it? This smart fellow is trying to batter down " Poor Richard's Almanac!" It is a fact; he is putting out all his strength to laugh out of American hearts the apothegms of dear old "Poor Richard." Those wise and pithy sayings, which Franklin found already in the hearts of his countrymen, and did not invent, but merely put upon their tongues, — these axioms unuttered till that great man came, — this cunning Britisher is attempting to repudiate by ridicule; and for what, think you? Why, to help British manufactures! That is the whole secret, found at the bottom of so

many of their disquisitions, not to say morality, —
the sly chap wants to get rid, somehow or other, of
Franklin's prudential adages, which have been ven-
erated for a century, and have contributed to the
good conduct of his countrymen, for the sake of bet-
tering the market in America for English goods!
Yes; all our ideas which regulate behavior must be
laid hold of at their very fountain-head in our first
principles, and turned into the channel of British
catechism, in order to widen and deepen the foreign
market in this country. So Kossuth tried to repudiate the " Farewell Address," to let in his doctrine
of American intervention in the Hungarian affairs.
Who would have thought of tapping American
human-nature so far back? Why, they will inter-
polate their ideas of the necessity of British workshops into American primers next. But hear him.
" We have an intense antipathy to the mean apothegms which we occasionally see quoted, we pre-
sume, from the margin of Miser's Almanac," —
meaning Poor Richard's, — " Waste not, want
not; " "a pin a day is a groat a year; " "a penny
saved is a penny got; " " there are forty sixpences
in a pound; and a pound is the seedling of a hundred." The reiteration of these axioms is, " Blackwood " says, offensive; and they sound like the maxims of a scavenger. This comes drolly from a
schoolmaster who is reported not to be backward in

their practice himself, whatever he may now pretend and urge for the sake of selling his work abroad. But let that pass. He proceeds in the spirit of a *drummer* to observe, " that one coat in the year may be sufficient to cover your nakedness; but, if you can afford it, by all means get three or four." Certainly every foreign manufacturer says that, for is not it for the benefit of the trade? " You have the comfortable conviction that you are contributing to the support of a score of excellent individuals, including the farmer, manufacturer, (*both in England*,) and Snip the tailor, who looks to you for his daily cabbage." There, the moral philosophy of this haberdasher in " Blackwood " is here enforced, and by himself. He tells us in plain language that he wishes us to buy and wear out as many English clothes as we can, because we thereby help to support their farmers, manufacturers, and mechanics. And for this the wise and time-approved maxims of the immortal Franklin, that true representative of the Yankee nation, the American Socrates, are to be brought into disrepute, and our principles of economy contaminated at their source.

MUSCLE.

E have frequently, and very lately too, taken occasion to introduce and urge the subject of MUSCLE, and the importance of cultivating its powers. We do not mean the muscle that was found in Jersey creeks two or three years ago, but quite another sort, yet bringing to its fortunate possessor a pearl of more worth than any found by the most lucky of the muscle-hunters in our waters.

If any excuse is needed for insisting frequently on the high value of good muscles, it is supplied by the fact that to make people sensible of the importance of their generous development is about as difficult, and requires nearly the same amount of repetition and persevering exhortation, as to effect that development itself. The strengthening of the physical faculties is admitted to require long and constant exercise; but it really seems to require no less persistence to convince people actually of the truth of the assertion, so far, at least, as to persuade them to act upon it in their lives. A considerable number may be made to believe that the exercise of the muscular system may improve it somewhat, but few out of the whole can be practically convinced that it will in any valuable degree be made applicable to themselves. If a man, they think, happens to be constituted by nature like Dr. Windship, the strong man of Roxbury, who is said to be *all shoulders*, it may be well enough to try to render those shoulders stronger by their perpetual exercise. In this way he is reported to have very recently augmented his power of raising with his hands weights from nine hundred and twenty-nine to ten hundred and thirty-two pounds, — almost a fabulous achievement for anybody, and especially for one said to be only about twenty-five years of age.

But still, it will be asked, What is the use of a narrow-chested, weak-shouldered man trying to shoulder a barrel of flour, lifting it from the ground as easily as if it were a water-melon or a bushel of potatoes ? The utility is, that this and similar athletic practices will augment the physical faculties and largely develop them, though perhaps never to such an extent as to impart the ability to raise a dead weight of eleven hundred pounds, or even to shoulder one of Bennett's enormous prize-pumpkins without difficulty.

Athletic exercises and the general development of the physical man have another value entirely distinct from that of rendering the body a powerful machine, — namely, the conservation of the health. But this is a topic often dwelt on, and we choose to confine our thoughts at present to the branch of the great subject of muscular cultivation on which we have just touched, — the improvement of the human body as a locomotive, an engine for labor, protection, and attack. The educated human locomotive can out-travel the horse, and its ability for instructed as well as merely animal labor is sufficiently displayed in the great productions which adorn or improve the world, from the Pyramids down to the Great Eastern. It is the feature of the human muscle as a protector and invader, that at the present period seems to claim a word of explanation.

The time has come in the increased liberty of men, especially of the American man, when the human muscle has attained a value never known before. In former ages, men's hands were manacled and their feet fettered by tyrants. What was then the utility of the strong arm, but to labor ; of the broad shoulder, but to bear burdens ; of the stout leg, but to run on errands at the mandate of despots ? That era is past, and the physical man is at length rising in the market, and even the black man participates in the upward tendency. The sinewy arm is beginning to be in particular request. For several years it has been obviously outstripping the intellectual part of the human organism ; it has at last attained a price at least on a level with mental talent, which it frequently surpasses. This price is a little uncertain, but is always high. As genius has no established market-value, so the pugilistic faculty has no exact quotation-price. This depends on fashion and caprice, just as the lecture of Mr. A will fetch a hundred dollars in the market, while that of Mr. B, of superior quality, will scarcely sell for thirty.

The muscle-power of the higher kinds cannot be had, however, at the moderate estimate of thirty, or even a hundred, dollars for an evening. A single night or day's use of a first-rate brawny arm — for it is a day-and-night machine, working equally well in both — will cost sometimes the price of a likely negro; and it is cheap at that in any localities; on special occasions, in Baltimore for example, and we may say not seldom in New York and Philadelphia too, a man cannot put his vote into the ballot-box, or even get the desired nomination of candidates to vote for, but with the useful aid of the muscle-power.

In the animal kingdom every one has observed that strength carries the day. The strongest ox, cow, dog, horse, rules the rest, and secures the first drink, the choicest morsels. The barn-door fowls obey this law, as well as the wild bird, the lion, and the tigers of the forest. Corporal strength is king

and emperor, without which cotton would be no better than coal ; and were man not stronger, putting
all his faculties together, than the strongest among
the other creatures of earth, he, with all his logic,
oratory, fine taste, and mathematics, would have to
play second, third, or fourth fiddle to the elephant,
the lion, or the tiger. The civil war which raged
in the early ages with those fierce beasts is over
now, but man had to fight hard for the mastery.

That contest with brutes being ended, a civil
war has broken out between man and man ; and
the strong man, hitherto kept down by the artifice
of despots, appears to be getting the upperhand,
especially in the United States, where they are
making the experiment of trying to keep society
together and improve it by reason, and not by force
nor fraud. We shall see ; if not, our posterity will.
In the meanwhile, as we have said, muscle is looking up ; the article, from fair to middling, is in constant demand, and the supply good. The hard
heads are looking down, as they eye their hard
hands and long arms, upon smooth beavers and kid
gloves. The dandies and exquisites are suffering
the greatest change. As a first step, they are
beginning to despise one another ; the next will
come soon, when they will have an equal contempt
for themselves.

THE HORSE-RACE AND BULL-FIGHT.

HE Exhibition of Horses near one of our cities, which lately so much aroused the attention of the public, calling up even the chivalrous spirits of the Ancient Dominion, accomplished many worthy objects, there is no doubt; but it failed to teach a lesson of humanity, so much needed, in the treatment of that noble, but suffering, we will not call him beast, because it would be derogatory to human nature, which in some respects really seems inferior. Since that assembly, where the horse was caressed and fondled by the beautiful and intelligent of both sexes, what has the country been called on to witness? A cold, deliberate, unfeeling, lingering murder of one of the choicest specimens of that helpmate of man which the world has seen! Would anybody believe, that, within a little month after the glorification of that creature at the festival on the banks of the Connecticut, men and women could stand by and witness the torture of the great Trotter on Long Island Course for the space of nine hours? Could it be credited, that, not content with that unparalleled performance, the spectators would be so inhuman as to suffer any brute to drive the overspent horse a mile further to win a bet, though all must have been morally certain that the feat would be followed by his immediate death ?

Americans may talk till they are hoarse of the cruelty of the Spanish bull-fights, — it is all gabble and sham. They love them; and there are multitudes who have assumed the name of American, ready to get them up without a moment's delay, if they knew how, or the public heart would tolerate the violation of morality. The attempt was made a few years ago to have a buffalo-hunt on the right bank of the Hudson, near New York; but, thank Heaven, the wild oxen smelt a rat, took to their heels and ran away, to the discomfiture of the gapers and gamblers, but not to certain speculators, we believe, who pocketed handsome ferry-fees and other substantial fruits of the adventure. A bull-fight is no worse than a desperate horse-race, like that to which we have alluded. It is no worse for a poor beast to be pitted in a death-struggle against another in the ring than on a race-course; to be gored to death by the horns of an antagonist, or to die by the bursting open of the citadel of life by compulsory efforts beyond his strength. To the speculators, it makes no difference. Those, too, who are capable of witnessing with satisfaction such a spectacle as occurred on the Long Island Course, would gladly attend a bull-fight, if they could, and oftener than they would the opera.

There is an immense amount of cruelty to animals in this country, which, though known well enough to some people, others appear never to suspect. But let it be understood that there is enough to disqualify the citizens of this Republic from passing judgment on cruel practices and sports in any other country; and particularly sufficient to shut their mouths effectually against denouncing the enormity of the bull-fight.

If there is to be any mortal running, we prefer to have the owners and backers of horse-flesh do it for themselves. And if there is to be any fighting to the death, we want Nicholas and Abdul Medjid to go to it personally pell-mell. It gives one a great deal of pleasure to have Yankee Sullivan and his competitor pound one another, not only because they both richly deserve a beating, but because this wholesome castigation of each other may save the backs or heads of some poor horses subjected to the violence and caprice of such base counterfeits of manhood.

CHANGE.

ITHIN a few short years almost every process, and every object also, has undergone a material change. An old burgher who had been absent five-and-twenty winters would not know Boston, New York, Philadelphia, or Baltimore on his return. The face of the country in many great particulars has altered. Hills, if they do not skip like lambs, as in the times of David, travel off to fill up hollows, or are levelled into plains. They are not safe nowadays, unless a monument is clapped upon them, as on Bunker's. Without some such protection none of the noses of the St. Anthonies are safe. Even Beacon has been condemned to bear houses instead of honors. In a few years Niagara will be yoked to the great water-wheel, and be seen grinding corn, as the Passaic has been for a long while making cotton cloth and paper.

They do not do anything now as they used to do. They neither plough, nor sow, nor rake, nor reap, as they did a little while ago. People do not work now; they look on and see the blackies and boilers sweating at it, while they smoke and play. Many men used to have many minds, and travel in fifty directions on a journey. Now they all go together to the same point. Great has been the revolution on the sea, as well as on the land. The free ocean has been enslaved. Brought up to the boiling-point, it proves a better servant than the wind, which is a chartered libertine at the best. Men waited once for wind and weather; these are no longer mentioned, except in some old almanacs.

A few things remind one of past times. The rain comes down very much according to the old fashion; but it does not wet one as formerly, on account of the India-rubber. And the thunder — ah! it sounds natural still. Never has there been better than some we had last evening. No deterioration or change there, thank Heaven! That thunder the rogues cannot steal, though Morse and others have the lightning. But there is enough left, as we also saw last evening, and of a beautiful rose-color, too. Let them turn the sun into a painter, the lightning into a postman, if they will. They cannot do anything with thunder, but to make bonny-clabber. After all, they are none of them so altered, but what we know them still. But Society, its habitations, pastimes, fashions, and employments — why, we hardly know them, unless

one's eyes are kept upon them daily, any more
than we recognize an infant in the brocade and
bravery of a maiden at eighteen. The face of
Nature changes rapidly, but that of Society out-
strips it.

The inhabitants of the earth used to live upon it.
They now live under it, down out of sight in cellars,
or else up where the birds once made their nests.
A quarter of a century ago, an exemplary man and
wife resided together with their children, like a
home-staying rooster, his mate, and chickens. You
will find them now packed up in hotels, where there
is no telling hardly one man's wife from another's,
as thick together as a flock of blackbirds, and as
noisy. Families are abolished, and Society is collected into flocks; but we are rejoiced to see the
barn-door fowl still sticking to his instincts — a surer
guide in some respects than reason, especially when
paralyzed by fashion.

But there is no end to these speculations, nor
pleasure in them neither; so we will only add, that
the face of Society is so changed that its best friends
cannot recognize the frankness and heartiness
which once sat so kindly on its features. In some
instances its natural expression is said to be covered
up by paint. The principal cause is feared, however,
to proceed from within. Were all well there, the

face of Society, like the countenance of the fallen archangel in Milton, would still be beautiful. It is the change at the centre of each individual, which has wrought so great a one upon the exterior as to render it not easy to recognize its ancient openness and simplicity.

STYLE.

THERE is a worthy gentleman who carefully reads all the advertisements in the paper; sometimes, indeed, he ventures a little further, but never to the neglect of these. As may be at once imagined, he is the possessor of vast erudition, and is better acquainted with the tastes, wants, ingenuity, and resources of society than almost any other person in it. Such must naturally be the consequence of so thorough a study of such a course of literature as he has for several years pursued. For the advertising department of a journal is the work of a great variety of authors, who understand profoundly the subjects on which they write, and who weigh deliberately every expression, because it concerns them in the tenderest point, their pockets. If advertisements are admirable for the correct and ample information they convey, they are in a special manner models of style. Strength of expression may be expected, and very figurative language is often to be met with, especially the favorite one of hyperbole, so common with Oriental writers. Metaphors are occasionally used, but similes are entirely rejected; for no accomplished advertiser ever can allow that anybody else has anything for sale at all like his own commodities, either in quality or fitness.

But political and moral writers may take a lesson from the advertising columns in conciseness, curtness, and idiomatic vigor. These valuable graces of style are cultivated, because these authors have to answer for every idle word in money; whereas the composers of the other parts of the paper fall into the opposite vice of redundancy from being the gainers by it. There is nothing like being obliged to pay for every line which one gets printed, to check a lavish flow of language. When tautology is an expensive sin, it is at once corrected, and repetition then becomes an unheard-of fault.

In consequence of these severe canons of criticism, the proprietor of a store of four or five stories, stuffed with goods of very great value, finds no difficulty in expressing his ideas concerning them, including a graphic description of the principal, — all in the compass of a dozen lines. Now, just compare these solid and admirable productions with the windy editorials on the opposite side of the leaf, or, if you want to see the most glaring contrast, put them by side of an eloquent speech of a member of Congress. There is a difference indeed! Speaking of honorable members of the Legislature reminds us to remark how much it would improve the style of speakers in that body, if a judicious plan could be devised whereby a small sum should be deducted from their pay, not only for absence from duty, but for gross expletives of language in their speeches, manifest repetitions, tautologies, and outrageous waste of good words, which convey no perceptible freight of ideas.

To illustrate the foregoing remarks, are added a few advertisements taken almost at random from the papers. The first met with, happens to be an example of what may be termed " business *blank verse.*" It sticks, you see, to the point, and is very sweetly expressed : —

Have constantly on hand, the usual kinds of Refined and Coffee Sugars and Syrups, viz :
Loaf, small and large loaves.
Standard and Circle A. Crushed.
Granulated and Powdered.
Clarified, whites and yellows.
Sirups, in hhds., tierces, and barrels.

The second, though comprehensive and full, is packed as close as such bulky articles will permit. Here it is : —

MACKEREL — Nos. 1, 2, and 3, in all kinds of packages.
SHAD — Nos. 1, 2, and 3, in   do.   do.
CODFISH — Dry, salted, and pickled.
SCALEFISH — Do.   do.
HERRINGS — Smoked and pickled.
PORK — Mess, Prime, Rump, Butt, Clear.
BEEF — Mess, Prime, and Railroad.
SMOKED HAMS, Shoulders, Beef, Bacon, Salmon.
CHEESE, Lard, Candles, Oil, Spices.

The next is a short specimen of the strong style, in which but one error is remarked, viz., " &c.";
and this, no doubt, originated in the best of motives — the worthy desire to abbreviate; —

> Churchill's augers bitts, and gimlets,
> Keith's copper tacks, brads, clout nails, &c.,
> Fitch's circular cap cabinet locks,
> Roy & Co.'s butts and snap hinges,
> Ward & Co.'s rules, box-wood, and ivory.

Here is a shorter and perhaps more vigorous one still : —

> Pig and Bar iron, gunpowder ;
> Blistered steel, ramrods, lightning rods,
> Spikes, bolts, hooks, and hatchets ;
> Clout nails, brads, and cut tacks.

Can anything in the classic authors excel the following in racy, unctuous, and, toward its conclusion, powerful expression? The length of the advertisement is forgiven for its lusciousness: —

Have for sale — Chow-Chow, Walnuts, Mixed Pickle, John Bull Sauce, Harvey, Essence of Anchovies, Reading Sauce, Essence of Shrimp; Walnut, Tomato, and Mushroom Catsup, Worcestershire Sauce, India Curry, Durham and Coleman Mustard, Schiedam Gin and Schnapps, Cette Port, Brown Stout, Cognac, Haut Barsax, Cote Rotie, Chateau Neuf de Pape, Monongahela Whiskey.

The last line in particular has a sounding rhythm ;* and the whole is instinct with the same inspiration with which Byron and Anacreon were filled. But this must suffice for a taste of the admirable condensation of the advertising style, its authors having the fear of the reckoning of accounts, and not of critics, before their eyes.

LETTER OF A DOG TO HIS BIPED
FELLOW-CITIZENS.

HEN I was a pup, men almost killed me with kindness; now I have grown to be a dog, they kill me with kicks or strychnine. Ladies then fondled me, stroked my back, tickled my head, warmed my cold nose, and sometimes even kissed me. What have I done to forfeit their love and protection? Yes; I am larger, that is true, and my teeth are stronger. What of that? I do not bite them. Boys get to be men; do women hate them on that account? No; I think not. Some stickle for principles, *not* men. They are for principles *and* men; and the ladies are doubtless in the right. But pigs are pets when pigs; when they become hogs, they eat them. So that we see again that circumstances alter conduct, as well as cases.

Why cannot I be permitted to take a walk along the street in summer without having my brains knocked out, or being poisoned by a midnight assassin? They represent that many of us go crazy in hot weather. All fudge. We display more sound sense in that season than our persecutors. Dogs stick to the city marrow-bones; while silly men and women are carrying theirs round all over creation, and don't get a market for them after all. The town is the place for bones, summer and winter both.

The inconsistency of men is astonishing. I was taught, for example, from my youth, to *speak* for a piece of meat when handed to me. And now, forsooth, if I offer to say a word to a man, even if it is the man in the moon, which I occasionally like to do, I am ordered to hold my jaw, and horsewhipped into the bargain, if I don't scamper. Is this fair? What is the use of throwing me into the dock, because I can swim, as everybody cannot; I do not like cold water because it does not happen to drown me; it feels as cold and disagreeable as if it did. Many men can swim, too; let's throw them over also. Why not?

Then making me run miles and miles, as I have done, after sticks on land and water; where is the sport, I should like to know? I have got brains enough to perceive its folly, though all boys and some men don't appear to have. If they suppose we relish the joke, because we *pretend* to do so, they very much mistake. It is nothing but a polite pretence on our part; a little hypocrisy borrowed from the fashionable society we frequent. Why, you must be simpletons indeed, if you imagine we run with pleasure after a dry chip, as if it were a bone. No; I, for one, am not so sad a dog as that. You don't catch me at such a game, any more than running after my own tail, like a miserable cat. A dog knows better, for he always runs away from his tail, especially if a tin pot is tied to the end of it by some son of a — gun. A sore finger to the scapegrace that did it to me the other day, is my sincere wish.

Oh, very kind, master takes me into the parlor. Yes, yes, very kind indeed; but it is only to be broomed out by mistress, who vows she will drive me away with a flea in my ear. Ah! the nice lady need not do that; I 've got enough already, which I ascribe to sleeping on the beds of her maids. Clean house that. I never stole a sheep in my life, though I am extravagantly fond of mutton, but I have been with my former master, when he did, and I was whipped unmercifully for it in his stead. For that I left him, and set up for myself, because I was unwilling to be punished any more for sheep-stealing, counterfeiting, cheating, or any other manly occupations. I have doubtless faults enough of my own; but hypocrisy and deception shall not be laid to my charge without an effort on my part to repel the calumny. I may brawl and fight, when provoked, as men do; but I do not, as they do, add stratagem to violence, and unite in one small skull the cunning of the fox with the ferocity of the tiger. When I want a thing, I get it where I can, — above-board I should prefer, though it is frequently thrown to me under the table. Out in the open air, let me get my living, breakfast, dine, and sup. I am willing to work for it, and do not insist on being an ornamental portion of a rich man's equipage to tag behind the carriage. Harness me in the milk or ashes cart; try me, and see if I am not an industrious dog. Read your books, I pray you; they testify in my favor. Learn from them what lives I have saved, whose loss would have rendered a noble line extinct or miserable; what joy I have thus brought to parents, relatives, and families! Read what pocket-books I have found of incalculable value; what thieves, robbers, and murderers among your own race I have ferreted out and brought to justice; what conflagrations I have prevented!

But I forbear; I will not boast. I hate all kinds of vanity and selfishness. Give me generosity, self-sacrifice, benevolence. These are qualities *after* my own heart, if not of it. I love to watch and guard the tender lambs, as in Landseer's " Twins," and dash out into the lake or sea to save the life of a human being, though he is often forgetful of the obligation and ungrateful. The world does not find our race most numerous among the wealthy; but we dwell in numbers among poor white men, Indians, and Turks. The reason is, that riches eat out the heart of Christians, so that we have to go to the Turk, the poor man, and the savage, to find it. Our lot is hard with the latter, but it is shared with the rest of God's creatures on terms of equity; and so we rest content. Anything is better than to be kicked and cuffed about the thoroughfares of civilization, as if we were stocks and stones, or no better than the poor sheep and calves which Christian men torture and suffer to be tortured as long as they live after getting into the butcher's hands, and then eat.

Oh! I have often cried, and whined, and barked to no purpose, to see these poor dumb creatures cut with cords, piled on one another, hanging head-downwards upon the wheel, that ground them like a grindstone, weak, faint, sick in hot weather, or stiffened with ice and snow. They who are guilty of these awful cruelties are certainly men, and profess to be Christians. But no dog would think of doing such things; if he did, a club upon his brain-pan would teach him better manners soon; perhaps poison would end him. I am truly thankful sometimes that I *am* a dog, and not a man — so fearful is his guilt, so tremendous his responsibilities. And yet he seems to be unconscious of them all. He knows enough to find out a dog's faults, and punish them severely, but overlooks his own. The strangest sight that we dogs ever see, is a man who is so inexorably exacting of virtuous behavior in our canine race, and yet insists on leading the very loosest of all lives himself. Demanding implicit obedience, he is at the same time an insurgent, sometimes in act, always in heart, against all authority, human or divine.

YOUR SLAVE UNTIL DEATH.

HASTE.

OBSERVE how poorly everything is done, when done in haste. The hasty man is the opposite of the quiddler, but there is little to choose between them. The former, indeed, brings the most to pass, but it is often good for nothing. The latter finishes well, but then there is nothing of it, after it is done. The character of a hasty man is certainly not worth affecting, and yet we often read at the bottom of a letter, " I am yours in haste, John Smith; " when, if the truth were only known, Mr. Smith composed it at his leisure. The real secret is, he wished the last words to operate as "errors excepted" in accounts, and cover a multitude of mistakes. " Yours in haste," forsooth. Such a man as Mr. Smith is not to our taste, by any means. We want no man's slipshod half-thoughts, born before their time, half-grown, half spoilt in the delivery.

A man in haste is, after all, very apt to be behind time, spending the whole day and half doing things in trying to overtake it. In consequence, he runs over little boys in the street; upsets chairs in the house; empties the inkstand, instead of the sand, upon his writing; tries to strike up a fire with his cigar, and puts the lucifer match into his mouth. If he writes for the press, he scratches off a hurried paragraph or two, in a race against time; if he is a shoemaker, his seams rip; if a tailor, the coat is sent home without any pockets. He catches up his cane, rushes into the shower, and has to return to fetch an umbrella. Legislatures in general, and Congress most of all, afford fine specimens, at the heel of a session, of labor done in haste, and how curiously the trait of haste is found connected in the same body, personal and corporate, with idleness and inertness. Congress, that can drag along through three months without a useful act, in the last three days loves to be heels-over-head in business. It is therefore just as impossible to tell what will come out of the legislative hopper in these last days, as it is what Signor Blitz will extract from a man's mouth or nose at one of his entertainments; it may be an onion, or a cabbage, nobody can guess.

The man of haste pays a ten-dollar bill for a turkey, takes one-and-eightpence for his change in silver and copper, and forgets the rest. He walks off with his poultry, boasting how cheap he got it. He puts his friend's letter, just received, into the post-office, and his answer to it in his pocket; sops up a puddle of ink with his handkerchief, and wipes his nose with the blotter; spoils a whole quill in attempting to mend it in a hurry; jumps into the river instead of the ferry-boat; puts his pants on hindside before, and his waistcoat over his coat.

Haste breaks glass and bones; ruins bank-clerks; makes holes in cloths and special pleading; produces war; gets a ship on the rocks, which it cannot get off, and a bachelor into matrimony, which he cannot get out of again. The hasty speech is soon cold again, — but not till it has lit up a flame in another's breast, that does not go out so soon; the hasty word is followed by slow repentance. Haste makes waste, hinders speed, and is to be recommended chiefly in cooking a beefsteak. In accomplishing anything, it uses the worst tools and the most expensive method, clutching at what is next at hand, is bad in bargains, to be avoided by the statesman, irreconcilable with grace and dignity in manners. It never discovered a planet, invented a machine or process, produced an epic, built a pyramid or temple, or fabricated anything designed to last. We know of nothing that is the better for haste, unless it may be a hasty-pudding and a hasty plate of soup; of which one must be allowed to be illustrious, and the other useful.

COOKS AND COOKERY.

THE celebrated French cook Soyer invests his rule for boiling a potato with so many qualifications as to be of little or no use to a practical operator in the culinary art. Nor can anybody make toast, it is affirmed, by his directions. One may as well expect to profit by formulas in grammar, where the exceptions from the rules are as numerous as the agreements.

The fact is that cookery is a matter of judgment, or rather an inspiration, not depending on exact recipes. The intelligent cook, as well as the intelligent physician, works by symptoms more than by science. The variety of combination in disease is infinite; it is no less so in cookery, where the process varies not only with the material to be used, but also with its quality, which is rarely the same. The cook cannot therefore act on precedents. His business is not a science, but an art. One must therefore be born a cook, and cannot be made one. His faculties may be cultivated, sharpened, improved; but his taste must be natural, it cannot be acquired.

It results from this, that, even in so simple a process as that of boiling a potato, a sea-captain, who was an epicure, was right when he remarked that not one cook in a thousand, no matter how high his pretensions, could boil a potato. Soyer himself could not teach it; he could only give some general hints, which after all required a cooking-genius to work out and apply. Says he, " It may be that they (potatoes) require to be put into *boiling* water, or maybe into *cold*, and either boiled *quick or slow ;* but this *you must find out*," says he. Alas for the poor devil of a mere " Secretary of the cooking-department, who gropes his way by the help of precedents which he finds on file," without the intuitive glance and insight of a Chatham of the kitchen-cabinet! How is a copier of other men's thoughts, the diligent and perhaps learned student of the books, ever to " find out " whether the water ought to be " hot or cold," or the potato boiled " quick or slow "? " Put a piece of lime into the water," says Soyer, " about the size of a nut, and some salt." What kind of a nut, how much salt, good Soyer? How is a man to know this, unless he has been born, not with a silver spoon merely, but a potato in his mouth, that is, with the faculty of discerning the spirits — the very different spirits — that inhabit potatoes? Judgment, dear Soyer, is what is wanted, as well as lime and salt, — and judgment, too, much bigger than a nut of any description.

Exquisite taste and judicial sagacity — these are the required endowments for a cook. And what an endowment do these qualities comprise for a single individual! The judicial talent, ample enough to fit its possessor for a seat on the bench of the Supreme Court, and the nice and delicate taste which, if turned to the pictorial profession, might exhibit to the world a Stuart, a Huntingdon, or Church. Do not then complain that a sauce is not well compounded, that a pudding has deficiences, a soup imperfections. Do not find fault even if the potatoes are not mealy. Rather thank God that you have any potatoes at all. If the devil sends cooks, just consider the difficulty of obtaining the almost divine faculty which is necessary even for the proper boiling of a potato, or the execution of a reputable toast. And can you expect that mental powers sufficient to qualify a man for a seat upon the Bench, or to hold the pencil of Michael Angelo, can be enticed into a kitchen, to vent there his glorious aspirations upon lime, salt, and potatoes, for the small remuneration of ten or twelve, or twice ten or twelve dollars a month? Alas, alas, it cannot be expected.

And shall we continue to go on as we have done, impoverishing ourselves with purchasing potatoes at exorbitant prices, which there is not talent enough in the country to cook? Shall we always thus remain in ignorance how to adapt to our use this precious gift from Heaven? One remedy occurs to us, but it is a desperate one, and is this. Draw off from strumming on the piano, the harp, and guitar some of those fine capacities which Nature evidently designed originally for excellent cooks, but are now prostituted into miserable musicians, often intolerable to others, rarely affording pleasure even to themselves. Could this project be accomplished, long before a new opera could be mastered, an amount of abilities would be directed to cookery — that most useful of accomplishments — sufficient not only to boil a potato and make a toast as they should be, but even to make some progress towards the invention of such a thing as a sauce, of which the United States is wholly destitute at present.

Among all the schools, academies, colleges, and universities, (bless the word, for that is all there is of it!) a school for instructing girls in housekeeping is felt to be a pressing want. They may talk of schools for sketching, painting, dancing, walking, — of lessons on the piano, harp, and voice, — some of them, perhaps all, have something to do in developing, moulding, polishing the mind and manner, and rendering woman agreeable, — but what are they, O ye graces three! when put in comparison with the glorious accomplishment of the fine art of Cookery?

We are all charmed, fascinated, by a lovely creature uniting the outside of a goddess with the interior furniture of a De Staël; still, even if she combine in that beautiful casket all the talents and acquirements of the nine Muses themselves, one thing would be lacking, one faculty indispensable to the complete and perfect woman, — and that is, the possession of the exquisite accomplishment of cookery. The other feminine acquisitions in science and the fine arts are of a personal, selfish nature; they set off the mind or body of the mistress of them to very great advantage; but they centre in the woman herself, and act, like the President's secretaries, as ministers of his will and pleasure. But the cook is essentially a generous, beneficent being, whose every action is for the gratification of others. Their pleasure is her loadstar — the everlasting object of her thought. It is this unselfish, sacrificing, expansive benevolence, that does not simply win upon and delight you, — it affects and absolutely subdues. No one can stand against the delicious invasions of the great cook who overcomes and entrances mind and body by her cunning manipulations, as Venus enveloped Æneas in her celestial cloud.

Yet daughters are never taught this victorious art. No one ever gives them a lesson on the subject. Their mothers don't, of course, because they are profoundly ignorant themselves. Nobody does, for nobody seems to know either its value or its beauty. We have spoken of the latter, but the art of cookery is exceedingly economical. You did not suspect this, did you? We thought so. Still it is very useful, we assure you; and a good cook can set forth a more satisfactory breakfast or dinner for a dollar, than an ordinary, clumsy, and ignorant, greasy gruel-maker would for five. But these last are tolerated because their employers know no better. There are no lady-cooks. The whole business of cooking remains almost as much a mystery to the mass of people as it was when bread was baked on hot stones, and meal was ground between two cold ones. Mothers don't know how to boil a potato, toast a slice of bread, compound a wholesome, yet toothsome sauce or gravy; how then should the daughters? Here and there is a family which has handed down the knack of doing certain things economically, sensibly, and agreeably. They are heirlooms, and have an indescribable charm. But nobody else catches the art; perhaps even the well-instructed family add little or nothing to the transmitted accomplishment. Still they preserve what they have received. And thus most excellent methods are in use in many a domestic circle, of which the world is ignorant, and likely to remain so till schools of instruction in the culinary art shall take the place of those for the culture of insipid tastes, of knowledge without any useful aim, and barren and sometimes hurtful accomplishments. The noble art of cookery is not to be learned in a cook-book, nor in Irish kitchens, nor genteel kitchens under Irish administration. It is one of the fine arts, in which *viva voce* instructions are to be given by those who know to those who can learn ; which lessons are to be illustrated by experiments, like any others in Natural Philosophy ; for cookery is a branch of physics, to be taught among the humanities.

We suppose that Heaven sends cooks, which is another phrase for *poeta nascitur,* for we demur to the common adage which makes this the work of the gentleman whom we would rather not mention. Heaven provides cooks as well as meats ; and those of the highest order are born cooks. They are natural, like the poet ; but they must be taught as well as the orator, who, by the by, is as natural a genius as the poet, notwithstanding Master Horace. The taught cook, however, is incapable of that freedom of flight, that richness of fancy, that belongs to the native-born. He will answer, however, for the present age and generation, who are as thoroughly delighted with eating their victuals served up in the unknown French language, as they are to listen to an opera in equally unknown German or Italian.

We have given this subject a prominent place, because we think it is more entitled to it than a message from President Buchanan, or a speech of Senator Toombs. And we could, if we chose, illustrate its importance by the example of Alexander Dumas, who has been travelling in Russia; for the first thing he did on his recent visit to Paris was to publish a work upon Russian Cookery. It is the art of arts.

You need not laugh at cookery, nor turn up your pretty nose, young lady, because we recommend it as a liberal artistic accomplishment for your sex; yes, the best of them. Find not fault with the injustice of the social system, as long as this useful and honorable department, requiring the best talents and skill, remains open to you; and what is more, remains unfilled. It is a fact, that, notwithstanding the pressing demand for cooks, even of moderate qualifications, they are not to be had. A lamentable dearth prevails, discreditable to the sex, injurious to the happiness of families, unfriendly to their health. The grossest ignorance prevails in some of the simplest and most common manipulations. How many girls employed in kitchens can stew an oyster, broil a steak, or even toast a slice of bread, as it ought to be?

Say not that this is small business. Nothing which concerns human happiness is trivial. Can that act be a trifle, beneath a man's or lady's notice, which is necessarily repeated three times at least every day, and every time productive either of our weal or woe? Do you say that cooking is doubtless an indispensable affair, and ought to be in competent hands; but that it is an excessively vulgar occupation, requiring a body's presence in the kitchen? And can anybody imagine that a lady is going to degrade herself by descending to that apartment of boilers, and onions, stewpans, and soap-fat? Let us tell this spirited and delicate remonstrant that a woman's, as well as a man's, place is where she can be useful; that she who thinks that her presence in her own kitchen, and occasional oversight of its work, degrades her, will also imagine that visits to the dark alleys of suffering, and the hovels of the daughters of want, are unbecoming. We never found your over-sensitive and elevated people, who were too refined to take good care of their own households, did much good in charity or sympathy to those of other people. What! are goose and gravy vulgar in the kitchen, and only genteel when upon the table, in company with dunces and lame ducks? Can that be low and unclean whose products grace our dining-rooms and parlors?

The manufactures of the kitchen call for the highest talents of the household, and are of a more complicated nature and higher rank than those by which the head of the establishment perhaps gets his living. Shall the gentlewoman of the drawing-room believe herself degraded by a little attention to a daily manufacture in the kitchen which is equal or superior to that business by which her husband supports her and his family?

Just reflect on what that culinary manufacture is; you will then attain some adequate notion of its dignity; its importance and necessity are every-where conceded. It combines several distinct arts or trades; that, for instance, of the confectioner, baker, and pastry-cook, together with a competent knowl-edge of chemistry, horticulture, agriculture, and natural history. We shall say nothing now of anat-omy and conic sections required in the process of carving. With all these arts and sciences, the lady-cook should be well acquainted, in connection with as fine an instinct and natural taste as would qualify her for writing or criticizing a poem or painting. Cookery a vulgar thing, to be consigned to menials without acquired education or natural genius! It is preposterous!

This country will never be what it ought—nei-ther its constitution, nor that of its inhabitants pre-served — without a more competent kitchen-cabinet than now exists. Such a body is now, as it has always been, as essential to the general welfare as the cabinet of the parlor. The finest talents, both of men and women, have been called into requisition by the demands of cooking and the kitchen. We are not so well acquainted as we ought to be, and wish we were, with the illustrious authors on this noble science. Mrs. Glass, Miss Leslie, Dr. Kichener, Monsieur Soyer, and Careme, are some of them. It is the noblest of the arts, and familiarity with its laboratories is an honor, not a disgrace, to any woman.

Cookery is the distinguishing characteristic and glory of our race. No animal but man possesses cooks. Take them away, and what have we left —but a munching creature of raw turnips and clams! The Republic would soon crumble into ruins if deprived of this its principal support, just as a house would tumble over if the kitchen were taken away. Your third, fourth, and fifth stories are excellent in their way; but the first floor is the main stay, after all is said and done.

If the vocation is thus useful and indeed necessary, it ought to be practised with judgment, discretion, and an eye to health. More lives are lost through bad cookery than by the cholera. When they are not actually sacrificed outright by ignorance, they are shortened and rendered uncomfortable while they last. A good cook and the doctor cannot flourish together in the same house; one will certainly expel the other. If you want to enjoy good health, you need not throw physic to the dogs; but give them all badly cooked provisions: the physic will follow of course. With an accomplished wife and cook, united in one, a man will live out all his days, and sleep soundly o' nights. He has found the genuine and only elixir.

THE EGOTIST.

DID you ever note the man whose standpoint for viewing every question was himself? — "That railroad is the worst for its management in the country. The persons about it are the most impudent and ungentlemanly." So he says. Now, what is all this tirade for? Why, on looking into the matter, — and to do so, little else is necessary than to hear the angry individual himself talk, — we say, that, after all, it is found that the man once thought he was not treated with sufficient deference by one of the conductors. That is the flimsy foundation for his judgment, and the provoker of his unwearied malediction.

Just stop a moment and observe his conversation. He speaks well of few persons who are not his toadies; and, though his opinions are bottomed on the most frail and one-sided notions, as the specimen given shows, yet he is just as obstinate in his persistence as if they were grounded on a demonstration of Euclid. As often happens, the amount of his prejudice is in exact proportion to the narrowness of his vision.

This man is incapable of deciding upon matters agreeably to principles belonging to each distinctly and appropriately. If he differs from another on the prohibitory law, thereupon he contracts a disgust at his opponent, and tries him on other subjects, as if they were somehow or other connected with the liquor-question. The reason is, he is so egotistical and opinionated as to be blind to any view of a subject which he has not taken himself. It is the word I, — the least one in the language, but yet so large as to shut out almost every other when placed beside it, — it is this word, so contemptible frequently in reality, yet so omnipotent with the selfish, that causes multitudes of small men to believe, or to act as if they believed themselves to be the nucleus or centre of the universe. Number One is a great number, and is represented by the letter I. These Ones are so numerous as to be reckoned by thousands.

There was an individual of this description who made up his mind that mutton-chop is the greatest dish there is, especially for breakfast. On this he continually fed, till he thought, as he was very apt to do, that his muttons ought to be everybody's muttons. One morning, he invited a young lady next him to take a piece, which she civilly declined. Thereupon he remarked, in a very severe tone, that he should not have made the offer had he not known that it was the fittest thing for her, which she ought to take, and that he was not in the habit of recommending what was not the best. Here were impudence and rudeness with a witness; yet nobody was in the habit so much as he of talking of *the gentleman*, and branding others with being no gentlemen, — his favorite phrase. His insolent language hurt the lady's feelings, and she wept, with suppressed anger however, it should be said. The trouble with this mistaken man is, that he has always one eye fixed admiringly on himself, while his other eye is — also paying homage to the same dear object. Could he, though loving chops extravagantly, not keep them to himself? More especially, whatever he might think proper to do with *mutton* chops, the fellow ought to have spared the lady from being insulted with *his own*.

Dogmatism, indeed, is the essence of such a character. Everything is considered as it touches him. Pleasure is not pleasant, unless he enjoys it; virtue is hardly virtuous, if it does not belong to his list of excellencies. Light itself is purer to him when refracted by his particular atmosphere, and nothing is exactly as it ought to be, till it is crushed or expanded into his standard. When another indulges in something, it is either vulgar or vicious. If he allows himself in the same, it is an elegant freedom or an eccentric taste, that accompanies genius. He cannot place himself in another man's shoes, if he should die. To this there is one exception: he stepped with pleasure into the old shoes of a rich relation, who deceased and left him a fortune.

EFFECT OF THE INCREASE OF GOLD.

[WRITTEN IN 1853.]

HAT are called laws in political economy are very different from those which pass under the same name in natural science,— astronomy, for example. These are so invariable and exact, that mathematics can deal with them as absolute certainties. Not so with those which are said to govern the growth of our population, for instance, or the effect of the addition of the gold products of the mines of California and Australia to the quantity of that metal already in existence. A law of rise in values has, however, been attempted to be deduced from the comparison of prices at various periods before and since the discovery of the Mexican mines, about the year 1500. It is assumed that the stock of the precious metals then in the world was a hundred and fifty millions of dollars. By the opening of those mines, it is computed that at the end of that century five times the original stock, or 750,000,000 dollars, had been added. In the next century, ending in the year 1700, an equal sum is supposed to have been contributed to the circulation, making the amount of the precious metals in possession of mankind to be fifteen hundred millions. In one hundred and fifty years more, that is, in 1850, this sum, by the operation of the American mines, had been augmented, according to a common estimate, to three thousand millions of dollars ; a few have placed it lower, and several, we think, considerably higher. But precise accuracy in the amount is not the point with us at present.

Now, it has been thought that there is a fixed proportion between these regular increments in the amount of the precious metals and the values of commodities and land. Thus, according to this theory, if there are now three thousand millions of dollars in use, property must be twenty times as valuable as it was at the discovery of America, three and a half centuries ago, because the gold and silver now in the world bears that proportion to what it then possessed.

But if the foregoing statements have any good approximation to correctness, no such law as has been supposed can possibly exist. For there has been no such change in prices. The price of wheat has been said by Smith and others to be the best standard for comparing the prices of all commodities at different times. Yet the discovery of the mines in America had no considerable effect on the prices of things in England for more than seventy years. It was not till after 1570 that a marked alteration was noticed, and that was twenty years after even the rich mines of Potosi were discovered. From 1570 to 1640, silver sunk in value, so that it took from six to eight ounces to buy a quarter of wheat, which might have been had before for two. Between 1630 and 1640, the effect of the discovery of the mines appears to have been completed, and the value of that metal seems never to have sunk lower in proportion to corn than it did about that time. Afterwards and during the last century, it continued to rise.

What, then, becomes of a law which claims to regulate the values of all commodities by the scarcity or abundance of specie ? — one which has excited the apprehensions of many, lest the abundance of Californian and Australian gold should almost have the operation of producing such a repudiation of its value as to make it by and by but a little better than a sort of " old tenor " of continental memory. The history of the discovery of the mines about the year 1500, and of its effects since, will allay all fears on the score of the immense appreciation of all descriptions of property.

In the first place, assuming the present quantity of specie to be three thousand millions, the annual addition, even from the present prolific sources, is but a small percentage on the whole. But then its depreciation, which we see must at any rate be very gradual, if there were no counteracting cause, is checked and almost entirely counterbalanced by a demand fully equal to this supply, bountiful as it is. While men feel its stimulating force in the increasing pulsations of business, the value of money cannot fall; indeed, a scarcity is rather to be apprehended from the rapidly growing demand. It may well be feared that the new uses found for it will very much outrun the imports from the mines.

When the wealth of a country increases, and the annual produce of its labor becomes greater, a greater quantity of coin becomes necessary to circulate a greater quantity of commodities. If we were a stationary people, and did not enlarge our industry and exchanges, while cargoes of gold were pouring in upon us, the effect would be widely different. But our enterprise, on the contrary, still shoots ahead even of our multiplied resources; and the fresh additions of the latter are, after all, inadequate to the execution of our grasping plans. Plate, pictures, statues, sumptuous furniture, luxurious houses, expensive jewelry, rich wardrobes, wines of fabulous age and flavor, equipages, and the like extravagance, will drink up the gold dust like so many sponges; and if there is any of it left, some of us will gild our houses with it as the Chinese do their pagodas.

For ages, other countries contributed gold and silver to that rich empire; but they did not lose their value, for the consumption was in proportion to their receipts. The very increase of the inhabitants of the civilized world demands annually a large fresh supply of coin to keep the stock of circulation good in the hands of every individual.

Beside, the annual contributions, amounting from a hundred to a hundred and thirty millions, more or less, will probably be stationary at about that figure, but by no means larger, while the whole amount in circulation is of course growing greater; thus diminishing the percentage of the increase of every year, till it comes to be a fraction not to be appreciated. But this percentage ought, in fact, as has been said, to be reckoned, not only on the specie used for the medium of exchange, but on everything else which is taken as money and goes to swell its amount, such as bank-notes, bills of exchange, and other negotiable paper. How soon some of these may be withdrawn from fulfilling the functions of coin, we do not know. What some administration through the country may attempt, no one can tell. Should bank-note circulation be forbidden in obedience to a delusive notion popular in some learned financial quarters, there will be a mighty vacuum created, which it will take California some time to supply.

On the whole, if any one is nervous on the prospect of a plethora of gold, we invite him to dismiss his fears. We assure him there is no present danger; and if he does not live longer than Methusalah, we believe it will not come till he also shall be gathered to his fathers. There is also a moral as well as a consolation : do not invest too deeply in land or anything else with the expectation of reaping an immense fortune from its rise in consequence of a fall in the value of gold. The present values of land and rent are evidently speculative. The actual abundance of the precious metals has not produced them, but the crazy cry of anticipated inundation, which, after all, will never reach us. Your speculator has a nimble fancy.

THE INTERCEPTED LETTER.

A GENTLEMAN sits in his gay saloon,
    In his easy arm-chair,
And probably would be quite alone,
    Were a lady not there.

Why standeth that daughter, tearing a rose ?
    Why so anxious looks her hound ?
How angrily, too, that father throws
    Uneasy glances round !

He is chiding, O fie ! his pretty child,
    For a letter of young love ;
She does n't look sorry, that maiden mild,
    Though detected, — the sweet dove !

The father is preaching of being discreet,
    And all that sort of thing,
And holding aloft th' intercepted sheet,
    As if it concealed a sting.

Then he fumes and frets till his face grows red,
    But she only picks the rose,
And demurely holds down her pretty head,
    While her dog holds up his nose.

The fatherly lecture is quite a bore,
As such things always are;
So she makes up her mind — not, to sin any more —
But to keep it from dear papa.

THEY WOULD BE YOUNG LADIES AND GENTLEMEN.

EOPLE, as appears from communications of correspondents and otherwise, are just now thinking a good deal of the training of the young. We have been doing the same thing, and will now relate, as applicable to the subject, what we chanced to hear one day, and shall entitle it —

THEY WOULD BE YOUNG LADIES AND GENTLEMEN.

" Where 's your father, Margaret ? "

" I suppose he 's in the shop, sir."

" Always hammering away, summer and winter, from morning till night ? "

" Yes, sir ; father is very industrious ; I really believe he works because he loves it."

" And where 's your mother, Margaret ? "

" She is in the kitchen, sir ; mother does so like to cook, and wash, and sweep."

" That you and your sister Harriet rarely have a chance at the griddle or the broom, it is likely."

" Oh, never, sir. We take care of the parlor, which, but for us, would have no tenant."

"You and your sister are, then, my dear, your parents' lilies of the parlor, who neither sew nor spin ; but continue to be arrayed as beautifully as Solomon, by the sewing and spinning of others."

"Sir ? "

"And your brother Henry, does he blow the bellows, or play second hammer to your father ? "

"Oh dear, no, sir ; he never works; he rides or promenades, goes to the theatre, and visits the ladies. And we go to the play, receive the gentlemen, and take a drive, or walk."

"And what do you do the rest of the time, for I suppose there is a little left ? "

"We are getting ready, sir."

"This really seems a very nice and pleasant arrangement — to three of you, at least. Doubtless it is all agreeable to your parents ! They like their end of the yoke, do they not ? "

"What, sir ? "

"Your father and mother like the arrangement which you speak of, — they are content to take their dividends of life in work? They prefer to labor themselves, and don't seem to mind if other people are always idle or not ? "

"Oh dear, no. You can't imagine how proud they are of being busy. They would not be doing nothing if they could, I really believe. Father was unwell a week some time ago, and idleness seemed to weigh upon him as much as his disease. He was glad enough to be active again once more, I assure you."

" Perhaps his unremitting labor is necessary to enable him to maintain his family ? "

" Why, perhaps it may be. I 'm sure I don't know."

" In that case, it is possible that when his income is stopped by illness, he may not be entirely easy in his mind; his prospects may not be clear and pleasant."

" I don't know how that matter may be, sir."

" But, of course, if anything should happen to prevent your father from providing, there is your brother, and he might " —

" Ha, ha! What, brother Henry? He can't split a stick to kindle the fire with, and does not know how to keep it going after it is made, unless it is to let it go out. Brother would rather have both hands chopped off than see them spoiled with work. He would die before he would let Christopher Cherrywit or Tom Tweezer know that he ever touched hammer or spade. And as for his sister and me, you don't imagine, I hope " —

" Not at all; there is not the least need of your doing anything, I see."

" That is it, sir. The old folks would not be easy without labor; they have never known what it is to rest and be amused, and we are ignorant of anything else. So we are both suited. Work seems to be their only delight; and it is lucky for us that it is so. Don't you think so yourself, sir?"

We did not hear the reply, and this heartless dialogue, of which we had accidentally overheard so much, was cut short suddenly at this point. But we got the main idea of a certain class of worthless youth, who make some figure in the world in their showy outside-surface way, — which is that people are like land under the old theory of farming. It must be smartly worked one year and lie fallow the next at least. The notion of many young folks now appears from this conversation to be, that one generation, namely the one now upon the stage and passing off, must do all their own work and that of the rising one into the bargain. The latter represents the fallow year. What is to become of their children? Perhaps the passing generation's tillage may suffice for two. At any rate, they will not trouble themselves about the matter. They trusted to luck and the labor of others themselves; their offspring must do the same. The art of slipping easily through life is, to avoid the rough places and shirk its difficulties. They can sleep, and eat, and dress. There will always be careful people about, who don't seem to mind, but absolutely to relish trouble; who would rather work than not. These will see that the doors are locked, that the fire does not go out when the rest of the household does, and that the stockings are mended, if nothing else is.

There is an enormously great fault somewhere, or these young and vigorous parasites would not be seen sticking to the old bark of past generations. Where is it? Is it in parents? have they eaten sour grapes? If they have, they have set their own teeth on edge, and not their children's. If exemption from labor is a privilege, children are gainers from parental tenderness and indiscretion.

Parents have doubtless eaten largely of the fruit of that tree of knowledge, which has cheated them into the belief that work, so honorable in the last century, confers disgrace in this, and therefore is fit only for the old. The rising generation, too much like the tide, which falls as well as rises, yields willingly to this theory of work, if it did not invent or import it. Sons and daughters are not ashamed to eat the bread of idleness, earned by the failing muscles of their parents. In reality, they ought in justice to change places. Young people should bear the heat and burden of the day, that the father may repose in the shade, and the matron sit by the hearth-stone to receive the guests. But this state of things is now quite reversed. The old man works all day to bring home something to his family, while his boy toils all night to spend it. The mother moves about the house intent upon domestic cares, while the vigorous daughter, almost invisible in silk and lace, occupies her seat in the parlor. The first thing that this young lady ought to do is "to rise up and call her mother blessed," and do what she can to make her so.

LARGE NOSES.

PHRENOLOGISTS make great account of the nose. If any one is disposed to set them down as dreamers, then we will cite Napoleon and other good judges, who thought very highly of this member, as a prominent mark of character. By them a large nose is considered an almost never-failing indication of strong will. One can see this every day exemplified on very common occasions. The first time you have to cross a ferry, take the trouble to notice who first rush out from it to jump ashore. They are all big-nosed people to a man! You need not take anybody's word for this, but examine for yourself.

It was not for nothing that a conquering nation of antiquity had *Roman* noses. No timid people they, who did not know their own minds. They knew them very well, and made the rest of the world acquainted with them too. Well-developed noses do not indicate predominance of imagination. The Romans were not distinguished for this faculty. But they appear, in some way or other, connected with taking the lead in practical matters. They go before, and clear the way, where organs of less size and strength would fail to penetrate and open a passage. They go ahead at fights and fires, and are foremost in crowds, in riots, and daring undertakings; sometimes getting the whole body into trouble; but then the first to lead the way to an escape. We see them pointing the way to glory in the warrior and hero, in Washington and Wellington; and, with never-failing forecast, guiding the sagacity of statesmen, the Burleighs of the cabinet. Cases there are, no doubt, where they have tempted men too far, as for instance, John Tyler into Texas, and Sam Patch overboard. But even in those uncommon instances, other noses, almost as long, have helped them out again. Taylor and Scott, with highly respectable endowments in this particular, came to the rescue of their big-nosed brother, and Sam Patch's ultimate fate itself is by no means an exception. His nose had brought that recklessly adventurous man to the surface many a time and oft, and given him breath; till at last, tired of being thrust always forward in such scrapes, it left him in the lurch.

We do not know if it has ever been remarked that the Hebrew nation owe their uncommon excellence in music to this portion of their physics, rather than to their ears. It is customary, we are aware, to speak of an ear for tune, an ear for time, &c., but we would suggest with deference, whether it would not be more correct to say, a nose for harmony and song. Certain it is, that the descendants of Jubal and Asaph are among the chief musicians of this day, as the illustrious characters we have mentioned were of theirs; and they are all remarkably endowed with the nasal organ. Evidently, the nose was not placed in such proximity with the instruments of vocal sound for nothing! And it is not only an index of musical capacity in its proprietor, but an excellent musician of itself.

But we have been in the habit of looking on this member as holding a higher office still than a prompter of the will, or trumpet for the voice. There is abundant reason to believe that it officiates as a rudder to the mind, and some notice that one who is making up his judgment, lays his forefinger for direction on this organ. Where judgment is predominant, there we are almost sure to find a nose of excellent symmetry and dimensions. There are those who scan the forehead and other portions of the skull to discover this controlling faculty; but we measure, on the contrary, the promontory between the cheeks, and pronounce our verdict on the character according to the result. Look then through the courts; we are not willing to go lower than the Common Pleas, and should not indeed incline to rest the question there ; but ascend to the higher judicial seats of the several States and of the Union, and, our word for it, you will see such a collection of noses as will fully reveal the reason of the acknowledged eminence of the judges of America.

We happened the other day to be examining some antique statues that have lately come to light. Among them were those of two great men, renowned in all ages for wisdom and penetration. They were the busts of Tacitus and Seneca. Both these sagacious persons, it appears, were remarkable for nose !

Having spoken of a few of the excellencies of this distinguished member, it may be expected that we should proceed to point out some of its attendant inconveniences, — such as its liability to be pulled, and others. But for this invidious office we have little relish. Beside, in our opinion, many of them are more fanciful than real. The one just mentioned, for example, is entirely without foundation. Such a nose, as we have honored with the epithet of large, has too much good sense and judgment to get into a situation where any one would wish or dare to wring it. No, no. It is your snub-nose that has now and then been taken between the thumb and finger to atone for the malversations of its master. Why, such a desecration of a nasal

organ of judicious dimensions, it would be beyond
the power of any ordinary digits to perpetrate, even
if they had the courage.

This noble feature has, however, been condemned
to indignity and suffering from human hands. Not
content with the stuffing and stifling it with the
most villanous of noxious weeds, men call upon this
single innocent member to atone for the sins of all
the other parts of the body. It is obliged to suffer
in public for the most disgraceful of secret vices.
Beside, though it never touches a drop itself, it carries about into every company the beastly tokens
of the drunkard. So true it is, that, let one member of society lead ever so blameless a life, he must
expect to suffer with, and oftentimes for, the rest.

SELF-MADE MEN.

E are heartily tired of this hackneyed phrase, which, after all, means nothing in particular. What a remarkable man is Mr. John Smith! and he is a self-made man too! Stop, friend! All men are self-made, or else not made at all — only half finished, as multitudes of such folks are. Calhoun and Clay and Webster were all self-made men; yet two of them went to college, and the other went behind the counter. Now it is perfectly well known to those who have spent four years within the walls of a college, which some make such a noise about on purpose to awaken jealousy, that everything there depends upon one's own almost unaided effort. The same devotion to individual culture exhibited outside those walls, will be followed by the same advancement and success with the great superadded advantage of being then styled a *self-made man*. This distinction is unsound, but it is one which the individual thus facetiously styled *uneducated*, because he has not earned a degree, has no occasion to regret. He

has been an immense gainer by his very depriva-
tions, since he is called the architect of his fortune;
though he is no more so than others to whom that
credit is denied.

Great talents have undoubtedly often lain forever buried in obscurity. To quote from a poem
which has touched all hearts, and from which the
arrows of small critics have ever fallen harmless, —

> " Full many a gem of purest ray serene,
> The dark, unfathomed caves of ocean bear;
> Full many a flower is born to blush unseen,
> And waste its sweetness on the desert air."

But where intellectual flowers have been brought
to light, thrown off the load of poverty that kept
them down, and had an opportunity to expand,
they have done so, whether found in a workshop or
in an academic hall. A college is not, as those
who have not tried it think, a hot-bed that will
turn a cabbage-plant into a cauliflower. A carpen-
ter's bench or an accountant's desk can work such
a miracle just as well as the wooden seats of the
recitation-room.

After all, self-culture is the only kind of education which will ever avail. No matter what school
or academy may have fed his early year with
knowledge, — no matter what Harvard or Yale
may have nourished his mature mind, — no matter
what learned lecturers may have, at least in theory,
filled up every chink and cranny of his brain with

science, and conveyed him around the circle of human knowledge, till he becomes dizzy with the journey, — still, after all is done, the *man* must fall back upon himself, cultivate and rely on his own resources, grapple with difficulties alone, and accumulate a capital of his own by his own solitary exertions. But this is being self-made, as much as a merchant or mechanic is who has risen to opulence and distinction. He too has had the benefit of the training of apprenticeship. Still neither apprenticeship to a merchant, a mechanic, or a college, will insure success and eminence.

A failure in these arises sometimes from want of inclination, more frequently perhaps from deficiency of talents. The last is a very common cause of failure, well understood ; but we are convinced that the former happens oftener than is generally suspected. Some of the finest intellects — we believe the experience of many who read this will confirm the remark — have little or no relish for the ordinary objects of ambition. In their half philosophic, half religious contemplations they pronounce the scramble for power and office vulgar, not worth an effort, and, when obtained, amounting in reality to nothing better than a voluntary assumption of hard work for the benefit of others. This, as they view it, may in conscience be sometimes incumbent on a man, and therefore not always to be shunned, but certainly has nothing so inviting as to be sought for by a person in his senses. To men of this organization, which is not so very rare, a voluntary lingering and persistence in the public service, however honorable it may be, seems very much like voluntarily becoming a plantation - slave. The petty honor seems to make all the difference; and what that amounts to, honest Jack Falstaff told us long ago.

The subject would not be complete unless it should be honestly remarked that self-made men are very often left unfinished, as if they had been made by Nature's journeymen, and not made well. Such imperfect specimens will pass in the tap-room, perhaps in the parlor, but will sink to a low level at the bar or in the Senate chamber. Your Colonel Crocketts are no doubt useful in their proper longitude and generation, but are as disqualified for many positions as Leatherstocking would be for the post of an alderman. They are all bad models for American youth, who may err in being too fine, but never in being too finished, and among whose numerous accomplishments completeness of attainments is seldom to be reckoned.

HALL–STOVE AND BROKEN PANE.

IN the hall are a stove and a window. The former is kept full of glowing coal; in the latter a pane is broken out, and it has been left unmended throughout the whole winter. What a wise economy is here presented! Yet it is of a piece with many a man's and many a woman's conduct during life. Good principles and habits may be conspicuous; but bad ones are suffered to go uncorrected. Virtues may abound, but so does vice; weeds grow apace as well as wheat, and it is frequently a question which of them will get the mastery. Sometimes the *broken pane* in the hall lets in more air than *the stove* can warm.

And one fact it is important to remark. Vice seems always perfectly able to take care of itself, while good principles need cultivation and care to maintain or multiply them. The cold wind will come in at the *broken pane* of itself without anybody's attention. But labor and vigilance are required to keep up a fire in the stove. The draught of the one is constant and perpetual, night and day, whether any one minds it or not. On the other hand, the stove-fire is apt to wane, and even go out, is almost sure to do so in the night, and needs incessant replenishing to enable it to maintain an equipoise to the blast from the window. Error, wrong, and vice are rushing in upon us in a ceaseless stream, whether we will or not; the equilibrium of goodness and the right is always in danger of being overcome. Indeed, this is pretty sure to be the issue, unless those evils shall be encountered by such bravery and stability of principle and good habits as shall oppose a barrier equal in strength and endurance to the assaulting forces.

The *Stove* and *Broken Pane* may be met with in various departments of life. When we see a man wasting ten thousand a year, while his business yields a profit of five only, the open pane and neglected hall-stove reappear to view. Another man talks loudly of temperance. It is well; but when he spoils his precepts by hard drinking, or opposes measures which can only really produce the spread of temperance, it puts us in mind of the broken window, which nullified all the good that the entry-stove could do. There is a multitude of people possessing amiable and valuable traits of character, but so tangled up are they with disagreeable habits and propensities, as to render them objects on the whole which one should avoid, as he would a bee who has honey at one end, but a sting at the other.

11

GREAT MEN.

IT is not easy to be a great man, any more than a great capitalist; but when once become great, it is not difficult to become still greater as well as richer. Men will lend their wills and money for you to sway and trade on. Everything and every opportunity combines to favor your increased influence and exaltation. Some men are great only because their cause is so. There is a moment at the turning of the tide when all is quiet and level around, and nothing indicates the movement of the waves in any particular direction. The prestige of greatness has not yet been attained. How small the apparent impulse of the tide at first! But when the preponderance in favor of the current has been established, how all the surrounding waves, as with one consent, tender their assistance, and rush on to bear him who rides upon the mighty current onward to his high destiny.

There is a calm in the atmosphere when scarce a breath blows one way or the other. Presently a slight motion of the air is just perceptible, and then all the winds of heaven seem to unite to send the blast of the hurricane along. Niagara itself was perhaps a rivulet no bigger than a pipe-stem once. When that had gained a passage, others innumerable, ambitious to follow their leader, pressed it onward, and increased its bulk, till it swelled into the river St. Lawrence, and attained a greatness, due not to one stream alone, but to a combination of many nearly equal. The Mississippi represents the way in which great men sometimes usurp all the credit, while some of it, and not unfrequently the greater part, belongs *rightfully* to others. If justice were done all parties, the Missouri would be more heard of, and the Mississippi less ; and many a general of an army, and chief of a party, would be cut down a head shorter, to put it on the shoulders of some of those able followers on which they rode into power and fame.

Men fall down and worship human greatness, which is as much their own manufacture as Baal, or the Serpent in the Wilderness. In the case of men who are really great, nobody is more astonished than themselves at the factitious importance given them by an idolatrous public. They know a little more, and can do a little better than most of their worshippers around ; and for this they, to their own surprise, are treated with sacrifices but little inferior to those offered to a heathen idol. The fact is that despotism seems a natural fruit of the human state.

Mankind voluntarily manufacture tyrants. These do not make themselves any more than poets. We must have somebody or thing to worship, and if we cannot find a king or queen to be the object of our stupid admiration, we will confer it on some general, orator, or demagogue, which many confound with demigod. When we have got the halter of a master round our necks, we feel easy, for we know then which way to go; and that's just as we are pulled.

How fortunate it is that one man cannot look into the brains of another; if he could, adieu to popularity and fame for superhuman qualities. How lucky one cannot look into another's heart; if he could, where then would be the confidence and subserviency of a party underling and tool? Well, there have been great men; but not so personally grand as poets and chroniclers have made them in order to comply with the exigency of rhyme and the interest of history. There have been good men, but not all of them so good but that others could equal them if they had a mind to try it. The memory is the most good-natured of the faculties, and kindly becomes a sieve to the defects, and a mirror to the shining qualities of the great and good who have preceded us. As to the hidden structure of men's minds, the differences are probably about the same as in the exterior shapes and dimensions of their bodies; so that there are few giants and no demigods on earth.

POST-PRANDIUM ELOQUENCE.

NE of the oldest and most noted manufacturers of brass clocks in the country — before his time they were made of wood — told us, that, sixty years ago, he managed by one artifice or another to keep his name perpetually before the public in the newspapers of that day, few and diminutive as they were. Sometimes he added a new cog, or wheel or two, or altered the arrangement of the old ones; sometimes the outside case underwent a supposed improvement. Now, the face was painted in a very striking manner, and again, it was an added hammer, that was made to strike. It was made to run eight days, fifteen, or thirty-one, (they make them go a lifetime now,) or only eight-and-twenty hours. No matter what the change, however slight, and often when there was none at all, the event must be duly chronicled in the weekly print. Such was his sagacity; and it was rewarded with money and reputation, and he became the most celebrated clockmaker in the land. Yet all the time, scarce a step was taken in the invention of a new principle, or even the improvement of an old one.

The New-England clock-maker is dead now, or he would have at this time competitors for notoriety, who would be an even match for him. What do you suppose the reason is that all the societies, of which there are some hundreds in the city of New York, take care to celebrate their anniversaries in public? It is the desire of their officers to get their names into the public papers, and of two or three of the members to be smuggled in also with their *well-conned impromptu* speeches, made at the accompanying dinners. Some men attend public dinners to put something into their mouths; others, to let something out. We know two men, one of whom never eats on those occasions, because chicken and oysters weigh down and cloud his wit, and prevent his shining; the other never drinks, for he says wine fevers his throat and makes his celebrated songs husky. Thus the itch to be conspicuous is favorable to the virtues, and in order to be flippant, one must give up flip. It is a common opinion that the love of talk, and especially the desire to see it in the newspapers the next morning, is the secret but genuine cause of the practice of public dinner-giving. Some men lecture; others get elected to legislatures; individuals are said to commit assaults and batteries, or kick up a row in theatres and ball-rooms; while others figure as professional, dinner, hotel, historical-society, and steam-boat orators, — all to gratify a natural, and therefore pardonable, ambition to appear in print.

The public must not be too hard with persons thus powerfully tempted. From considerable observation, there seems no reason to doubt that the ambition to be the subject of a paragraph is one of the most irresistible temptations of modern times. For the want of it, among the ancients, smart men stirred up wars, and grew into renowned generals, or else engaged in schemes to overturn the liberties of their country, or cut the throats of its tyrants. The modern vent for a great spirit is pacific. The types are a satisfactory reward for all his aspirations. Accordingly, in order to obtain their favor, one way is to trump up a sham discussion in the papers; another, to pick up some foreigner, and make speeches at him for awhile; and some have even been known to make a donation to a historical society of smoky or mouldy volumes, which had been encumbering the garret for a generation. These and similar methods are all worth trying; but they will not bear a comparison with the success of the table or impromptu orator. There is nothing the press is so eager and delighted to pick up and preserve as what falls from a speaker's tongue, and *post-prandium* eloquence is always of the very best quality, catching a flavor, no doubt, not from Helicon, but the distillery. Nowhere does patriotic fire, or love of woman, or the press, glow more intensely. These are the standing themes, enlarged on sometimes till the speakers are compelled to sit. The sentiment, *pro aris et focis* — or, as translated by the cockney, our *arts and halters* — will never cease to have a relish at anniversary feasts as long as men shall honor the one, or deserve the other.

This remarkable disposition to be distinguished as speakers lessens the wish to be recognized as actors. Your speakers and your actors are not often the same persons. Great barkers do not bite. Perceiving this, the American people have a practice of sending to Congress delegates principally eminent for their powers of protracted speech. Being unfriendly to over-much legislation, they take good care to select such excellent orators for their representatives and senators as will be pretty certain to spend the time in talking, so that the Republic will be likely to receive no harm. It is certainly much to the credit of this faculty and practice that it confers such reputation upon the possessor, at the same time that it does no injury to any one. Who can quarrel with that which does no harm, while it tickles the vanity of so many who would on the other hand be miserable if they could not talk, and at the same time be talked of? Talk,

talk, talk, is the conservative element in our system, the true brake, breeching, or holdback in the body politic. If the honorable senator could not vent himself in speeches, he might do some mischief; take away these hindering buckles and straps, and away the car of state might rush down-hill into the gulf — of Mexico, or some other as bad. It is better to let people, especially those in places of dangerous authority, enjoy the full play of one uneasy member, than, by curbing it, turn the whole of the entire man to a terribly serious action. Men must have some place where they can be looked at, and be famous. If not allowed to clap their wings and crow upon their own dunghill, they will sally forth, like Burr, and go to conquering another.

SHORT MEMORIES.

MEMORY appears sometimes to bear a certain relation to the dimensions of the body. Some have grown up so high, no wonder they are unable to remember anything that happened at a time when their heads were on a level with those of other people. Boys, the children of the rich and influential especially, when ripened into men, have very unhappy memories. They can hardly ever recollect any of all those "eternal friendships," contracted in their early days, when they associated for years with their intellectual superiors of the poorer classes. We have remarked that a boy "brought up at college" is rather more unfortunate in this respect than others, forgetting everything which happened before he entered; and if a lucky chance should afterward, when he has left it, throw him into a city pulpit, there is not the least probability that he will ever be able to call to mind one of his old village acquaintances, even that with the farmer's lovely daughter sharing in the common decay. We have heard of the still more remarkable case of a charming girl, who unhappily lost her memory so entirely in consequence of her father's touching $50,000 in Norwich and Worcester in a month, as to forget a whole circle of more than a dozen of her " dearest loves " the very day she heard of it.

There is in our nature a beautiful antagonism to this phenomenon. It is called into exercise and observation when a gentleman of opulence is reduced by some of the many untoward events of life to the reflections of poverty. This accident is found to be an extraordinary tonic to the faculties generally, but to none probably more than the one we are speaking of. Such a person has forever afterward a very clear remembrance of what he once was, and can even relate all the particulars of his former splendor, — a proof of the wonderful *vis medicatrix* that penetrates our poor humanity.

On inquiry, we have ascertained that short memories are very common indeed. There is a proud family in the neighborhood of Washington Square, whose heads cannot remember such a personage as a grandfather on either side. The offspring of parents inheriting homes erected from the proceeds of quack medicines or patent blacking, are almost always afflicted with shorter memories still, hardly recollecting who their fathers were. Fashionable citizens who have spent a whole summer most agreeably in the midst of a sensible and cordial society in the country, are never able to recognize a soul of them on meeting them again next winter in the city.

There is up-town a very fine aristocratic gentleman of fortune made by judicious investments during the early part of life in old clothes and reputable haberdashery, who seems quite at a loss how he came by his property, but is rather of the opinion that it was derived from an ancient entailment in the family. Indeed, we scarcely ever met with an instance where a man who lived to ride in his own coach ever remembered to have trundled a wheelbarrow, except that of the late Benjamin Bussey, in his lifetime one of the millionnaires of Boston. We have often heard him boast of the humility of his origin, and of passing his early years as a silver-buckle-maker and itinerant tinker among the hills and valleys of New England. Great men will sometimes recur with pride, and gratitude perhaps, to the meanness of their youth; but such an avowal must be looked for among rich men very rarely indeed.

This capricious faculty begins to falter in some quarters at an early age. People who have passed their grand climacteric are expected to be visited with failing memories of course; but the puzzle is that this sad disaster should overtake so many, especially if single, about the time of their arrival at twenty-five or thirty. Miss Prudy and Mr. Primrose are severally fifty, to say the least; yet though neither of them ever dream of cutting that figure, they would cut from it if they could. They cannot call to mind a single event that happened more than fifteen, or, at the most, twenty years ago. The family record is unaccountably obliterated by some mischance, and there is positive danger of their forgetting even the day when they were born, though celebrated so unwisely in their unforeseeing youth, but fortunately the interesting dates are indelibly impressed upon the memory of every woman in the parish. O that time, like merit, might be kept from advancing by forgetfulness or neglect!

When this defect prevails, as it is said to do sometimes, to such a degree that husbands forget their spouses, and *vice versa*, and even become liable to take those of other people for their own, it ceases to be merely ridiculous or unfortunate; it rises then to the dignity of sin, which must of course be turned over to the clergy, as better conversant with such matters. Still we must say that it will hardly do to carry benevolence to the pitch which some do, who deem it incumbent on them to treat other persons exactly as they do their own family.

After all, there is a whimsicalness about this subject which deserves to be particularly noted. The very same person who labors at one time under the malady of a feeble memory — when he borrows a sum of money of an acquaintance — will at another, when he happens to be the lender, perceive that the faculty is singularly strengthened. One gentleman, with whom we are acquainted, is a striking instance of this kind of tide in the power in question. He is in the constant habit of repeating the names of all his rich connections to the fraction of a cousin, but never for the life of him can recall even so much as a niece or uncle among all his poor relations. We are ourselves a proof of this strangely intermitting faculty; for we perfectly know the inestimable value of short articles as well as pastry, yet are too apt to forget it when we take pen in hand.

Notwithstanding this we must adventure just to add to the present article, that there are cases still more extraordinary than any which have been mentioned. They exist where a man in the possession of the shortest of all memories forgets himself. This was the misfortune of the dashing Dick Drivebays, when he broke his promise to marry the noble Clara for the sake of the wealthier Miss Beaumond, who, on hearing the baseness of the scoundrel, told her maid to say she did not know that individual. A more distinguished example occurred, when gentlemen in Wall Street, who on other occasions are universally acknowledged to remember remark-

ably well if they choose, actually lent Mr. Walker
five millions of dollars, notwithstanding they knew
there stood close behind him the devil's imp of a
sub-treasurer, holding a box to put the silver in.
Egregiously as they forgot themselves on that day,
we don't believe they will fail to recollect the circumstance for some time. It is thought that the
Washington financier got credit as well as cash in
that transaction, and proved himself such a match for
Wall Street, that the financial department will go
on quite easily as long as its Secretary is a Walker.

We are tempted to extract a moral from all this;
and though everybody must laugh to see his sober
visnomy in such a place, we hope it will be forgiven
with the same good-nature that we are in the habit
of showing toward the clerical temptation to let off
a pun in a sermon. The lesson is this: seeing
therefore the exceeding shortness of the recollective faculty in human nature, don't distribute your
property to your heirs, nor suffer the rogues to help
themselves to it, till you are under the sod. If you
do, the sooner you are there the better; for they
will forget such a little circumstance even before
those shoes of yours, which they have stepped into,
are half worn out. Make them, if they need it, a
generous allowance, and the chance is possible of
being remembered sometimes on a quarter-day.

CHAMPAGNE.

CHAMPAGNE! Champagne!
How like a snake it sparkles, hisses,
And, as a lying Judas, kisses,
    Flashing amain!
Gods! who would taste such poisoned blisses?
Who is the cursed fool that wishes
    The cup to drain?

Champagne! Champagne!
Fill high! aye, fill your deep-mouthed glasses,
And, as around the venom passes,
    Ring out the strain!
Io Bacche! come here, ye asses,
Ye drunkard-wrights, who still molasses,
    And God's own grain!

Drink we, friends, so well met here,
Drink we to the absent dear,
Drink we to an early bier,
    Io Bacche!

Ye whom a doubt perplexes,
Ye whom a sad thought vexes,
Drown conscience, that distresses,
    Io Bacche!

Whose fond heart hath felt a blight,
Whose love-star hath lost its light,
Drink, and quench your soul in night,
    Io Bacche !

Pledge true hearts and love-lit eyes,
Pledge our friendship's golden ties,
Pledge the worm that never dies,
    Io Bacche !

    Champagne ! Champagne !
Poet ! whose songs make pimpled faces,
And Bacchus ! who our race disgraces
    Lower than Cain !
Oh ! would that you whole calabashes,
Brimful of punch and brandy-smashes,
    Were forced to drain !

    Champagne ! Champagne !
Pah ! the filthy work advances,
The staggering furniture enhances
    Delirium's reign !
How silly are Tom's drunken glances ?
Before his glazing eye-balls dances
    A hellish train !

    Champagne ! Champagne !
Now with the clustering grape-wreaths bind us,
Our noble landlords all remind us
    Not to abstain !
Hold ! ere this vine-shroud has entwined us,
We swear ! that none shall henceforth find us
    Sober again !

12

THE FAST MAN.

WHO is this celebrated individual whom nobody can overtake? Even Time himself, swift as he is represented, may be taken hold of by the foretop; but the Fast Man shows nothing but his back, as he is outstripping all pursuers. He is undoubtedly an American, who can run through ten miles or a fortune quicker than anybody else. Certainly he sails the fleetest ships, and drives the steamer the most rapidly. Who eats so quick as he? The Americans are the greatest riders in the world. Hiram Franklin is now turning the Parisians dizzy with his round of circus-feats, — thereby perpetuating the fame of the philosopher of the same name, still remembered in the gay capital of France. For the Parisians adore genius, and do not much mind whether their homage is paid to a conqueror or a cook. Eaton Stone — their very names betray their Yankee origin — is likewise vaulting into the saddle of celebrity in London, and riding and *reigning* in the admiration of the people.

The Fast Man must certainly be an American,

because nobody lives and propagates so fast as he; and if he is so when wide awake, be sure he is when fast asleep. If he falls short of being fast in anything, it is in this, that he is not quite so steadfast as would be for his good. See how he spends! If he once sets out on the road to ruin, no one can make an end of the journey sooner than he. But if he can run to the devil with greater expedition than any other man, it is but justice to acknowledge that he can probably run back again with similar speed. An American funeral is sometimes seen upon a trot, and, if patience alone sits on a monument, our countrymen must be content to go to the grave without one. Of course he has, from a mere feeling of impatience, been obliged to apply steam to navigation and invent the telegraph. Neither could he possibly submit to the old slow way of cradling his wheat and other grain crops; so he invented McCormick's " Reaper "; and that men might not die any longer in the slow process of one at a time, Colt has presented us a " Revolver," which will settle the matter for a dozen at once. An American is not slow at breakfast; so attached is he indeed to creature-comforts, and so well entitled to the appellation we have given him, that in some States a particular day, called " Fast," has been set aside for the special accommodation of tho Fast Man, and on it his execution at the table is double the usual rate.

The diseases of the country assume the characteristic type.　We hear but little of slow fevers and lingering complaints ; galloping consumptions are the rage, and the old quaternian can't be found in Webster's dictionary ; and so we suppose it has either become extinct, or been converted into a daily fit. In one part of the land at least, the city of New York, extraordinary haste has been exhibited to leave the world.　Children who have just come into it, stay but a year or two, before they are in a hurry to depart.　So great is the universal love of progress through the country, that even candidates for office, who won't run, are dropped immediately. Such a thing as a stand-still is utterly intolerable. No constitution of any of the States can be suffered to rest for more than ten years or so, when it is marched off at double-quick time to make room for another.　The temper of the people has affected the language ; for we cannot suppose that a lady actually conforms her naturally graceful pace to the common phrase of her American gallant, when he invites her to " trot out " with him, and give her friend, Mrs. Wing, a flying call.　In communities so active, one must make up his mind to meet much hasty temper as well as pudding ; but it will be no great matter if the proper sweets are added.

One thing more : however fine it may be thought

for boys and girls to leap over the barrier that divides them from gentlemen and ladies, — however flattering to national pride for America to be running the race of empire in her early youth, — the judicious, whose eyes have been placed in the forepart of their heads on purpose to see where it is best to step, and so that they may look before they leap, will not deem it improper to quote, for the benefit of fast people, the old Latin maxim, " Festina lente," — *make haste slowly.*

TEMPTATIONS OF THE NIGHT.

THE evening air of the country is considered to possess a noxious power; that of the Southern States especially is known to be poisoned with deadly malaria. The night-time in town is not a whit more safe than it is in the forests and meadows. Its atmosphere may not be loaded with such fatal vapors, and ghosts may not squeak and gibber, as in village church-yards; but the paved highway and the purlieus of gas-lights have small immunities to boast of in this respect, for the devil himself takes his nightly city-rounds in person, and does not delegate his business to inferior spirits.

The immoral nocturnal malaria of overcrowded seaports is more to be avoided than any swamps or rice-grounds whatever. What fever can be compared with that tide of hot blood which surges within the veins of thousands under the pale influences of the moon, in whose potent beams even dead fish and flesh are said very soon to lose their sweetness and contract a taint! What chills of soul succeed the debaucheries of these unholy and tempting hours of darkness! Most of the licentiousness, drunkenness, gambling, and sensual indulgence occurs when the light of day, together with the pure spirits that inhabit the sunbeams, have departed. The bad spirits of the lower world appear, if at all, when the good are gone, and have always been feigned to walk the earth, when thus abandoned, as it were, of heaven. The night is then no time for man to be abroad. If the stars and planets have a voice, as Addison says they have, they warn us, upon their nocturnal rising, as plainly as the tolling of the curfew-bell, that, the labor of the day being over, it is time to retire, and be out of the way of doing or receiving mischief in the obscurity of the approaching hours. Instead of obeying, however, the heavenly voice, — as it may be termed, for it comes from the heavenly orbs that roll above us, — the setting of the sun is a signal among thousands that their day is but just breaking. Many have slept all day to be fresh and ready for the evening party or carouse. The theatres throw open their vomitories; the gambling-hells and drinking-pandemoniums are illuminated as by a midnight sun ; and the brothel sets its snares. Opulence glittering with silks and diamonds, gold and lace, wakes the echoes of the streets, disturbs the tired sleep of the industrious, and disperses the fevered dreams of the sick, as they pursue their noisy way, during all hours of the night, to ostentatious jams, given for the display of the good luck of recent speculation, and frequently paid for from the shallow funds of approaching bankruptcy.

We have no holidays, they say. How should there be, when every night is spent in dissipation? One hears no appointments now for pleasant intercourse in the daytime. The inquiry is, Where shall I see you to-night? And the reply is generally, at some theatre, or oyster-cellar, or subterranean, lower yet.

Such was not the custom among our virtuous ancestry. With them, day was a time for pleasure, as well as toil, and night was a season for domestic enjoyment and rest. Those good people thought the sun and moon had made a sensible division between the night and day, and knew which was which. The multitude now believe they don't know anything about it, and that what was formerly called night, is day, and the reverse.

Notwithstanding this, however, we have inherited so much of the spirit of former times as to be of opinion, that, if a kind of curfew-bell law could be established, by common consent, without its ancient tyranny, and people were to go to bed and put out their lights, not, as then, at eight, but at ten o'clock, that this one single regulation would dispense with half our penitentiaries and police-force, — purify or else annihilate the theatres, shut up most of the dram-shops and gaming-houses, and reduce crime and pauperism to be manageable evils. Night-tides are the highest. Those of passion in the human soul are no exception; they belong to the great system of universal influences. Fountains, dry by day, have been known to burst forth afresh at night, and there is a night-pulse pervading humanity wherever it is found, aggravating fevers and all diseases, and often rendering them fatal in spite of skill and care. If there is not an unseen but omnipresent enemy abroad when darkness overspreads the world, then poets are silly dreamers; for they have universally spoken of the activity of such nightly agencies unfriendly to our race. Some of them appear even to have owed to them no small share of their inspiration. As evidence of this, volumes almost might be quoted; but we shall mention only the song of Thomas Moore bearing the title of " Fly not yet," in which he entreats his companions to

> " Fly not yet, 't is just the hour,
>   When PLEASURE, like a midnight flower,
>   That scorns the eye of vulgar light,
>   Begins to bloom for sons of night,
>   And maids that love the moon.
>
>   .   .   .   .   .   .
>
>   'T is then their soft attractions glowing,
>   Set the tides and goblets flowing," &c., &c.

He continues, —

> " Fly not yet, the fount that play'd
> In times of old through Ammou's shade,
> Though icy cold by day it ran,
> Yet still, like souls of mirth, began
> To burn when night was near.
> And thus should woman's heart and looks
> At noon be cold as winter brooks,
> Nor kindle till the night returning
> Brings their genial hour for burning," &c.

This is from one who knew, so that we cannot doubt of the temptations and unhealthy nature of the powers who rule the dark hours of the twenty-four.

THE NOVEL-READER.

COUSIN Hatty is an enthusiast in that branch of domestic industry known by the name of "light reading." One night, after being rapt in a volume of this description till nearly twelve o'clock, she shut it up, exclaiming with animation, as she did it, "Oh, Thomas, where *should* we be, I wonder, were it not for books?"

"Abed, I suppose; where else *ought* we to be, my love?" answered her husband, looking softly into his young wife's attractive face. — [*Bibliog.*

THE dying candle burns dim,
   St. John's is tolling one;
Zoneless and slipshod the maiden sits,
   A speechless statue of stone.
From morning's blessed light
   To noon's meridian glare;
From mid-day's splendor to black midnight
   She sits like a spectre there!

Read — read — read,
   Magazine, novel, and tale,

With sateless appetite reading on,
  Till the brain begins to fail.
Is it strange she is so pale,
  Her eyes so heavy and red,
Her raven hair so faded and snarled,
  Her languid blood so dead ?

A worm is gnawing her heart,
  The book-worm, hungry and lean ;
Twin-born to him of the fiery still,
  With fangs as cruel and keen.
Books — books — books,
  Conceived in labor and pain,
Vampires ye are of body and soul,
  Whose ruin is your gain.

Health, and comfort, and friends
  Yield to your serpent-charms ;
Love, husband, child, are forgot,
  To clasp you within her arms.
While suffering sighs unheard,
  While poverty pines alone,
She weeps over fiction's tender page,
  And makes feigned sorrows her own !

O God ! that a creature so good
  As woman at her prime,
Should peak and shrivel on such vile food,
  So long before her time !
She might have a serious soul ;
  She might be at forty a belle ;
Why need she live a frivolous thing,
  Whom sense becomes so well ?

Tales — tales — tales,
  Duty, reality, truth,
Are only fit for grandfathers now,
  Too homely things for youth.
When stories are swallowed down
  As histories in disguise,
How long ere history will become
  But a story in our eyes ?

Men once saw the devil in Faust, —
  The imp at the present day
Still handles types, but never before
  In such a devilish way.
In power he 's stronger than steam,
  Swift as the lightning in speed,
Ink-black, though fair he may seem,
  And talks like a lawyer fee'd.

This demon, subtle and false,
  As once in paradise,
Laughs in his sleeve to see the sex
  Taking his good advice.
He tempts them with numberless tomes,
  Duodecimos and octaves,
Where love-sick Fanny in woodlands roams,
  Or moon-struck Manuel raves.

Beware ! great reader, beware !
  The rankest fancies of men
Have scattered poison everywhere,
  By the power of press and pen.
The worst that ever was thought
  Is stamped on the printed roll,

And she, who has gained all books have taught,
  Has lost a virgin soul.

Still, 't is heaven, she thinks, to read,
  'T is hell to sweep and stew ;
Millions are born to suffer and slave :
  She — she has nothing to do
But drop an indolent tear
  For beings who never lived,
And break her heart for a ruffian in print,
  Or a Miss in fancy deceived.

So dreams the novel-sick heart,
  Weak literary thrall ;
Ah ! the soul that thinks only others' thoughts
  Is hardly a soul at all :
It is but an echo, or shade,
  A parrot, ape,— what you will, —
An intellectual duplicate,
  Not worth the room it may fill.

Past midnight, — still she strains
  Her eyeballs over her book ;
Still zoneless and slipshod the maiden sits,
  With a wild and haggard look.
From morning's wholesome breath
  To noon's meridian glare ;
From mid-day's beauty to grim midnight,
By solar ray and pale lamp-light,
  She has sat, a spectre there !

THE PROFESSION OF MEDICINE.

THE circumstance adduced by superficial thinkers to detract from the DIGNITY and USEFULNESS of PHYSIC, constitutes in fact one of its principal claims to consideration. We allude to the multitude of medical charlatans. Where there is an abundance of sharks, be sure some valuable fish are near. It must be a noble vocation which invites numerous pretenders. There are few counterfeits of a worthless bank ; and a miserable author, or school of art, invites not many imitators. It is a rich soil that is most infested with weeds. We want no better evidence — though it is true we have it — of the value of the professions of divinity and law than the shoals of fanatics and pettifoggers, that, like vermin upon plants, contrive to get a sorry living upon some of the branches of those noble trees of knowledge. If they were less deeply grounded than they are in the wants of man, there would not be a tribe of hangers-on deceiving and depending upon them for subsistence. Parasites are only seen on the noblest growths of the forest.

It would be strange indeed if the five-and-twenty centuries, which have been flowing on since the father of physic flourished, had not in its thousands of streams brought down valuable deposits of medical knowledge to the present day. In that space of time immense quantities of golden sands have no doubt been deposited upon our plains, and large contributions of medical science have been collected and embodied in books. Diseases of every variety that have afflicted humanity during that long period have been diligently investigated, and the remedies and results recorded. Some have been subdued and disappeared; some prophylactics have been discovered, and all have been alleviated. If any remain incurable, it does not derogate from the claims of medicine to the respect and gratitude of mankind.

One cause of the want of a complete triumph of the healing art originates in the perpetual influx of new diseases arising from the new conditions to which our race is from time to time subjected. No sooner has the faculty succeeded in developing and ameliorating the old, than strange disorders arise, with which they have to struggle anew, and if possible to subdue them. Thus medicine makes continual progress, and can boast of numerous victories, but is robbed of much merited honor because fresh enemies spring up as fast as the old ones are conquered.   This gives a stationary appearance at times to medical science, and sometimes of being even retrograding.   But such a conclusion is unjust.   As well might the complaint be made that charity is dying out of the world because the wants of the race continually multiply.   As well might we accuse astronomy and theology of going backward; for there never have been so many questions in either unresolved perhaps as at the present moment.

The fact is, in proportion to the advance of knowledge does the dark void of the unknown expand before us.   In the infancy of the world, all appeared plain enough, merely because so little was known.   Man has found ever since, that, as he rose to a greater height, his views extended farther, and yet the horizon that lay before him was become more distant than ever.   The science of medicine has only had the experience of other branches of knowledge.   The progress of the race, its improved circumstances in some instances, and altered ones in all, have brought in from generation to generation new phases of derangement of man's physical system for physicians to contend with.

The body of medical discoveries and principles has been steadily increasing, but not faster than new human wants demand, if so fast; and consequently the boundaries of ignorance seem not at all contracted.   The collection of facts and doctrines is immense and valuable, and is always growing larger ; yet they must necessarily lag behind the new demands for them which spring up perpetually ; and they must therefore at the time be more or less inadequate. But medicine has never been more enlightened and progressive than at the present moment, and its genuine progress never more honored, or deserving honor. As might be expected, it is at just this season of its prosperity, and because of it, that the richest harvest of quacks and nostrum-mongers, charlatans and dupes, is witnessed. It must be so; the brightest lights cast the deepest shadows. True science should not be disheartened at this, because it is the law of progress in mind, as well as physics, that obstacles of folly, deception, ignorance, cupidity, should increase in proportion to the rapidity of the advance.

SOCIAL CUSTOMS.

NE of the most agreeable concomitants of the prevailing prosperity is its diffusion, not only among the great but also among the little folks. It reconciles us to the sight of lordly palaces and splendor, to know that the *one-stories* have also enough and to spare. But that is not the point of my present writing, which is to let you into several of the new customs springing up in society probably in consequence of the fresh fields of pleasure which sudden and unexpected wealth has lately opened.

By far the most serious and delightful occupation in this city is the evening party, including the concert and the ball in that comprehensive term. It may be a little expensive, to be sure, as now managed; but what matters it at a time like this, if fortunes which are made in a day should also be lavished in a night? It may be a consumer of time as precious as money; but of that there is a surplus too; for some of us, who are young, have nothing in the world to do, and do it. Oh, it is so pleasant;

time never can hang heavy, with a party once a week, which it takes all the rest of it before and after in getting ready for or rid of.

INFANTS' PARTY.

And now these pleasant enjoyments are not, as formerly, restricted to people in their teens, but are wisely extended to — not those who are out of them, but to tiny pretty creatures, who have not yet reached them. I lately saw a card of invitation from a lady on the Fifth Avenue not quite *two years of age* to another Miss of a *little past one*, requesting the pleasure of her company at a *conversazione* in seven days thereafter. Thirty of both sexes were to be invited of about the same blooming age. I have not heard what took place at the meeting of these rose-buds, for the time appointed has not come; but we have no doubt, diminutive as they are, that they will blow out pretty handsomely, — they would not be New Yorkers if they did not. Each will go accompanied by an adjutant, of course, to attend to *necessary details*. As to the *conversation*, none of them being able to talk as yet, it will probably rise no higher than that of their older brothers and sisters on similar occasions.

We have been favored with an answer from one of the Misses, declining the invitation on the ostensible grounds stated in the note, which I am at liberty to send you ; — it will be found annexed. But I am privately assured that the reason of declination really·was that the little lady had lost a favorite kitten lately, and so was out of spirits. Going into company so soon after such an event was thought to be improper, even if she had not bruised the tip of her nose in falling into the washbowl.

" MY DEAR JOSEPHINE, — Please accept my compliments and regrets, that, in consequence of my mamma's prudential notions about young ladies going into society before they are out of their teens, (that is, they must be two years old, you know,) I must forego the pleasure of a romp in your mamma's fine parlors. Only to think of the fun of rolling and tumbling, fumbling and crumbling, smashing and crashing all the pretty things. I declare it is too bad ! when, in all my life-*long*, I have never had so rare a chance to exhibit my accomplishments that I should be prevented because I am not considered to be out of *leading*-strings. Ridiculous ! when I have *run alone* ever since I was a year old — last September. Then she thinks I require so much attention and a constant looking after ; but it is no such thing. I don't *want* so much looking to. I want to do just as I have a mind to ; and then I don't cry, nor kick, nor scratch.

" My mamma says I have a remarkable talent for mischief. Now what do you think she calls mischief? Why just the throwing of my great-grandpapa's miniature into the water, and washing the paint off his dear old face, which had not been washed for at least fifty years before. If that was wrong, why do they wash my face every day, I should like to know ? I don't like it at all, and they are aware of it, I assure you.

" I think this a very strange world. I don't understand half the things in it, though I am esteemed such a paragon of wisdom and cunning that my fond parents are sometimes afraid that I know too much for this world, and so will bid adieu to it and them, and betake myself to more enlightened regions, where genial spirits are waiting my angelic presence. But, dear Josephine, I fear I am getting what is called rather high-flown ; so I will just stop and bid you good-bye.

"P. S. — Is this not a rather *long* epistle, for so *short* an acquaintance ? if so, pray excuse it. I hope to learn curtness and pertness, and all that by and by.

"Yours truly,   Lulu."

THE DOG—PARTY.

At the risk of spinning this letter out tediously, I must inform you of another party, that has come to my knowledge, though I cannot arrive at the particulars. A lady, it appears, admits to her society a beautiful poodle, for which she has a high regard. One day she resolved to show this by inviting twenty-five of the handsomest and most agreeable fellows of the same race to visit her friend. They came, every one; not a single excuse was sent. There were crop ears and long ones; little puppies and great ones, as will always be the case at parties; white, black, and red; slender and chubby; of greyhound and bull-dog families; of long silky locks of hair, short hair, and none at all; generally with whiskers and moustaches; here a cur crept in and ran between the legs of a noble Newfoundland, and there a stout good-natured spaniel overturned several little fellows with his caresses; in short, there were twenty-five snappers and barkers of every variety. They were all fancifully dressed in ribbon streamers. I learned that they were regaled upon dainties they were fond of, and had been accustomed to be treated with, — for they were aristocratic dogs, — such as chicken without the salad, beef *a la mode*, sugar - candy, sponge - cake, and cream. One of these genteel dogs forgot himself so far as to put his nose into one of the cream-pots, and thereby soiled his ruffles; for which impropriety there was a general bark of " turn him out, turn him out," as usual among Bowery Boys; so he was sent home very much chopfallen. No other accident has been divulged.

JOHNTE.

BOSTON.

Who was it said, " Great cities are great sores ? "
Ah ! 't was a grave mistake, and many scores
That wily Southern statesman made,
Or else posterity belies his shade.
　　But 't is a falsehood base,
　　A libel on our race ;
　　And History shall give the lie
　　To the unnatural calumny.

I summon Lacedæmon, Athens, Rome,
The hundred towns of Greece and Italy, to come.
Ay, had you never bravely piled
Your mighty ramparts 'gainst the onset wild
　　Of rapine, tyranny, and crime,
　　A line had told our destiny ;
　　And at this distant time
The leopard's lair had been our savage home.

And you, proud mistress of the " silver Thames,"
　　With the pale Adriatic Queen,
　　The brilliant Regent of the Seine,
And all the stars of Tuscia's diadems,
Who o'er the trembling fugitives once threw
Your serried shields, when flying from the Vandal crew ;
　　I call on all to brand

The aspersion of your land,
And boldly claim
The meed of fame,
For civilizing man so justly due.

And shall the tributary verse,
Which feebly essays to rehearse
The well-earn'd praise
Of deeds of other days,
And glorious men of every clime,
Whose names yet swim upon the sea of time,
Forget the pride
Of Charles's winding tide,
Which hopes ere long,
With grand old cities side by side,
To be embalm'd in deathless song ?

So gracefully she sits
Upon her gentle heights,
She seems just lighted from her airy home,
Or risen newly from th' Atlantic's foam.
So sweet a summer sight may scarce be seen,
As Boston with her hundred islands green.
Then too her sea-built wharves and granite stores,
That line her docks, and fringe her ship-girt shores ;
Her lordly palaces round Beacon's haughty brow,
The " Common " spreading, like a lake, below
Its velvet robe of green,
Hemmed in between
Tall sycamores, and elms so old and grand,
By my own Brookline's scented breezes fann'd ;
Her solemn churches, shooting high their spires,
Lit up, like dying saints, with evening's fading fires.

The old Provincial Legislative House,
Which helped their fathers' patriot ire to rouse,
And separate a kingdom, now divides
But only State Street, which it gloriously hides.
The Quincy Market-House, and, more than all,
Young Freedom's Cradle, famous Faneuil Hall.

But not for these I lift my voice in praise,
They are the common themes of poets' lays, —
The casket merely, in whose bosom lie
The precious gems that miss the vulgar eye.
Far nobler subjects prompt my unbought song,
Her hearts to bless, and make weak virtue strong.
Her deeds of love — devotion to the laws —
And arms to strike in Freedom's sacred cause;
Her souls contented to be greatly good,
By princely spirit warm'd, if not by noble blood.
These, Boston, are your jewels, brighter far,
Than all which blaze in an imperial star.
Your Lawrences and Lowells, Perkins, Grants,
Your Tuckermans and Channings, struggling to advance
The weal of Boston, say you? or their State?
Oh, no; — 't is this which animates the falsely great.
No *Chivalry* — mean plant of selfish souls —
Their pure and large philanthropy controls.
Heaven, knowing how they 'd use the bounty, gave
To some the power, to some the will to save.
And, when vouchsafing men of fortune there,
In mercy lent them hearts that knew not how to spare.
We find one rich, perhaps another, kind;
The wonder is to see them here combin'd.
The ignorant and sick, the blind and dumb,
The sailor wandering in his floating home;

The poor of every nation, kindred, name ;
To them appeal, and — granted is their claim.

The Muse must pause, for were she to repeat
The deeds of Love in this her favorite seat,
The list would swell, like lawyer's bill of fees,
Or that of Greece's ships by blind Mœonides.
Boston, in fine, possesses all that's rare,
Except the proper article for *Mayor!* *

    * They could not choose a mayor for a long time.

FOREIGN TRAVEL.

HERETOFORE the majority of the people were well content to live happy and die at home; but a trip to Europe has been regarded, within a few years past especially, as one of the greatest luxuries and even accomplishments of the age.   It is inquired no longer of a gentleman where he was educated, has he a diploma? — but has he been abroad?   If the answer is affirmative, the traveller rises to par at once in the fashionable exchange, and takes his station in the drawing-room with acknowledged double Ds and reputed single *prima donnas.*

About the middle of the present century this tendency to the ancient world began to display itself among the cattle population of the West.   A select company of the beeves and swine of that polished region made an excursion to the country of their ancestors, and were appreciated for all that they were worth.   We all know the advantages of a European reputation; they rose immediately in public estimation at home, at Bull's Head and Brighton, and have been continually rising to the present hour.

A voyage to the Eastern hemisphere is indeed a compendious passage to public distinction, but attended with embarrassments. The salt ocean has its terrors. The travelling quadrupeds had therefore to be prepared and reconciled in some measure to the trial. With this view they were familiarized to brine before embarking, and thus preserved against one of the principal evils of a protracted sea-life. As for the rest, they were shipped in packages like the Irish emigrants to these shores, who find themselves well packed, it is true, yet somehow do not experience its saving power so effectually as could be wished; for hundreds of them, notwithstanding the pickle they are in, are lost upon the voyage.

Thus matters went smoothly on till a few years past, when people walking through their corn-fields were said to hear distinctly the words " We are sent for," rising up from among the hills ; while every ear of corn appeared to listen to the unusual remark, and the deep-green leaves fluttered with pleasure, and waved like the undulations of the Atlantic, though not the slightest breeze was blowing at the time. Similar ominous sounds, but in the Dutch language, were reported to have been heard in the wheat-districts of New York.

The burly farmers pondered in their hearts these singular expressions of the young blades, stuffed their hands to the bottom of their breeches'-pockets, and finding no light in that celebrated abode of it, said nothing. The next steamer brought the astounding news of the repeal of the corn-laws. The corn-fields over the whole country were ready for it. Warned, as we have seen, by magnetic influences, of events taking place in Europe, they made a speculator's use of the information thus obtained in advance of the mail, and grew as is well known with astonishing rapidity and evident satisfaction, day and night. Ambitious as kernels always are, in the general at least, and resolved that their western rivals, whom they had been the making of, should never go before them, with all their legs, they made up their minds to accept the first card of invitation that should be sent them from across the water.

But here was the rub. The other travellers to Europe that have been mentioned, had either acquaintances or connections there, or were descended from ancestors residing in that quarter of the globe. Indian Corn was therefore troubled with misgivings respecting her reception ; for she was an unadulterated indigene of America, without a drop of foreign sap running in her stalks. Really never tasted by Englishmen, she had the misfortune to be constantly in their mouths, yet only to be slandered. Though naturally modest and rather mealy-mouthed, yet these things vexed her, for she possesses considerable spirit, as distillers know, and can become quite snappish when thoroughly warmed up. Notwithstanding these disadvantages, however, on being strongly pressed by the good-natured queen of the Islands of the Sea, she hastened to shell out, and depart from her native soil along with her companions.

Their reception in Great Britain was the most flattering possible. The common people, the best judges of the productions of nature as well as art, received them gladly with open arms, and mouths also. All was joy; nothing went against the grain. Their introduction was instantaneous; they were absolutely devoured with kindness. The people could not get enough of them. The hesitation about Indian corn disappeared immediately, and the corn likewise.

After the grains had sailed, the potatoes regretted that they had not borne them company. Some reasons for that step might be weaker than in the case of those who were gone; but there were others in their favor of peculiar strength. They were out of health, and a voyage to Europe had been frequently recommended by the faculty to persons in that condition, particularly the clergy. It might be beneficial to rusty coats as well as black, who have been known to receive so much benefit from a voyage to the Old World as to be induced even to visit it a second time. There seems to be something in her worn-out constitutions that wonderfully renews their own. With such uncommon eyes, too, as Murphies have, no one could hope to see more of European manners and customs; but alas, their absence from their native hills could not be supplied so well as that of the clerical profession. Potatoes enjoy not the help of apprentices and journeymen to take their places in emergencies. The conclusion of the matter was, they were compelled to be content to remain at home, and snuggle together under their own vines, nursing their disease as they may. In the mean while, something surely ought to be done for the cruel rot which afflicts them. This obviously might be removed by added care, for this would turn it into carrot, which Dr. Underrow of the Farmers' Club assures us (and he, of all men, ought to know about everything below-ground) is one of the very best esculents for cattle with which he is acquainted.

Bills of mortality give the clergy credit from the days of Methuselah, who was probably one of them, down to Elder Harvey, of living as long as anybody need to do; yet there is no description of men among us who are so afflicted all their lives with periodical complaints as they. Ten or a dozen years of pastoral labor are sufficient to bring on symptoms so alarming as to baffle the whole *materia medica* of America, and render a resort to Europe absolutely indispensable. Fortunate it is that the malady which calls for so expensive a regimen chiefly occurs to those unfortunate individuals who enjoy a liberal income. The wonder is, how the other two learned professions escape the terrible disease. It is true, their business at home would be ruined by the prescription of a two years' residence abroad, and clients and patients might possibly object to pay for physic and advice, administered only by a figure of speech. For that reason, or some other, they are exempt comparatively from the twin scourges of bronchitis and dyspepsia; and instead of the luxury of the disease felt only to be cured by travel in foreign countries, they are obliged to put up with the compensation, however inadequate, of unremitted health at home.

The steward of an ocean-steamer discovers an insight into the real condition and wants of a valetudinarian, unknown to the faculty who practise on the land. It is he who commences the regenerating work which the inspiration of the air of the Old World is destined to complete. How different is this from the atmosphere of the New! No one can help acknowledging, on the least reflection, that air coming over the craggy peaks of our granite mountains must be entirely too hard and dry for the purposes of digestion. The fine moist atmosphere of

London, on the contrary, will dissolve our food almost without any trouble on our own part, — an interesting fact to dyspeptics. This is an important saving of human labor, and shows the reason why three millions of our race have squeezed themselves within those small boundaries. At the present time unusual accessions have been made from the Scotch and Irish countries, where the function of digestion is believed to be somewhat interrupted. It is hoped that the English climate will put it again in motion.

It has been reported by the most fashionable tourists, who are invariably the most critical amateurs of art, that the breezes which have the advantage of sweeping over the Pontine marshes possess qualities very agreeable to clerical invalids. In fact, their excellence is apparent in the immortality of Cæsar and Tully, who used to dwell in their neighborhood a great many years ago. Works of art also executed in and about Rome have lived so long a time that it is conjectured they will never die. There our countrymen bid fair to experience in a similar manner its embalming power. But this extraordinary influence will probably not be imparted to every traveller who pursues lost health in those classic regions. These find their principal relief in the studios and *conversaziones* of Italy, and salons and operas of Paris, under the care of female professors of Hygiene, who practise in these hospitals. The malady of the throat (sometimes called the clergyman's disease) is never able to resist their prescriptions in the French and Italian tongue, for any length of time.

But alas! the opinion of the most of those who have tried this course of treatment is like that of our Irish fellow-citizens respecting vaccination — that it wears out in a very few years. No sooner does the afflicted one venture to return to his native land, than the process of degeneracy commences, till another application of the remedy seems as necessary as ever. So the regimen is repeated, and always with success; and, whatever may become of his usefulness, life is sure to be preserved. So have I anxiously watched a battle between a spider (the disease) and a toad (the patient). Now the spider bites him in his throat or stomach; whereupon the poisoned toad with haste betakes him to a neighboring plantain, whereof having partaken as much as likes him, he, nothing daunted, returns to his first position, and renews the fight. A second and a third time the venomous insect strikes him with his fangs, and the blessed sea-green plant as often extracts the deadly virus from his fat body, and restores him safe and sound as ever to the combat. But when this wonderful panacea can no longer be approached, the poor sick toad yields him languishingly to his fierce distemper, and succumbs to inevitable fate.

THE LATE MAN.

THE late Mr. Onslow is not deceased, as might naturally be conjectured from the little epithet which always precedes his name. The expressive monosyllable is his by the fairest of titles, for he purchased it at a high price. To be late is one of the most expensive of luxuries. It cost the Orleans branch of the Capetian line the loss of the throne of France. But though the Count of Paris may or may not have missed the sceptre, from the tardiness of his grandfather's abdication in his favor, he gained a valuable device, which he and his heirs may wear instead of the lilies. "Too late" may be inscribed on his escutcheon in exchange for the inheritance of which the robber Louis has despoiled him, — an exorbitant price to pay though for two such stunted words; but mottoes have always been dearly, often desperately earned, — sometimes acquired by virtue, frequently by violence, and always at great cost.

"The late" Mr. Onslow is apt to be rather tardy in his movements, and never in his life knew what it was to be at the right place at the right time;

consequently never gained any victories, nor other advantage, like Lord Nelson, by being at a spot, or executing an act, a quarter of an hour before the time. His appearance or performance always happened a quarter of an hour after. Like a bad musket he perpetually hangs fire. Everything he touches seems to do so too. His watch is ever a quarter of an hour too slow; and its owner therefore is sure to be just where he ought not to be. He is always conjugating the verb " to be " in a future tense, yet can never overtake the present. Mr. Onslow has a son, which has been put down as the only evidence he ever gave of punctuality in conduct.

This unfortunate habit of Mr. Onslow is a sore inconvenience to him. Such a man can have no contemporaries; for he comes after the times of other people, and may be therefore looked upon virtually as a species of posterity. No person knows so well as he what it is to see the boat a good ten minutes upon its way, on his arrival at the slip. The comfort of being left behind by the cars, himself and bag and baggage, is a daily experience with him ; so that he is always regarded as a passenger in the next train but one. He probably never since he was born saw more than the tail of a procession, or heard anything but the peroration of a sermon. To him, therefore, texts are secrets, and the music of

life unknown, at least that part of it which marches
in the van of street-parades. Mr. Onslow probably
imagines that dramas are composed entirely of fifth
acts, having heard no other ; and was 'on one occasion astonished to be told that people had soup at
dinner, never happening to have come to the table
till the second course. He once tried his hand at
gardening, and projected a splendid melon-patch ;
but he did not think to put his seed in till he saw
ripe nutmegs in the market. There is not a kinder-
hearted man ; and he would be of essential service
to his friends in sickness, if he could only make it
convenient to call upon them before they were given
over by the doctor. His purse is ready for the destitute and suffering ; but nothing else about him is ;
so that his money rests in his pocket undisturbed,
till the poor object of commiseration is in jail or the
alms-house.

But this may more properly be reckoned among
the inconveniences which his tardy habits bring on
others ; and these are quite as numerous as those
they entail upon himself. To prevent a dozen people from transacting business, because he delays his
coming, is too common a circumstance to be noticed ;
for he never by any accident did otherwise. The
only time he was ever recollected to have arrived
in season was to attest the execution of a neighbor's
last will ; but it is confidently predicted, it will not

be possible for him to make his own. He is a strenuous politician and ardent party-man, but he is sure to get to the poll in a great fever just after it has been closed. If a lawyer, such a man gets his client nonsuited; if a physician, perhaps his patient may thrive by his neglect; if a minister, he is apt to keep the congregation waiting, not upon the Lord, but on himself. His note lies over at the bank just long enough to be protested and his indorsers frightened, when he pays it with the costs. His day is made up principally of afternoons, and he begins to count at eleven. He goes to market just in season to buy what everybody else has left, and has it sent home to cook after the fire has gone out, which reminds us to remark, that, when he was a fireman, he commonly met his engine on its return home. He buys an umbrella after the shower is over, locks the stable-door when the horse has been stolen, and places his pet flower carefully under shelter the day after it has been frozen. It is credibly reported of him, that, when he was a boy and went to school, from always being tardy, he began to learn the alphabet in the middle, and consequently found his appropriate place at the tail of every class, for which part he has had a strong predilection ever since.

What Mr. Onslow's calling is, we purposely conceal, as we would say nothing to impair the benefit of his bad example. What method can be thought

of to administer correction and reformation to faulty
persons of this description, we do not know.   What
if society should instigate another individual still
more lax and tardy than this grave offender — a
"later" Onslow, for example — to practise upon him
those very vexations and annoyances which he has
been so long inflicting upon all he has had anything
to do with?   To cure and prevent intemperance,
the Spartans exhibited a drunkard in his beastliness.
He who is plaguing everybody with his foibles may
be ashamed of them perhaps when he views them in
another.   If the late Mr. Onslow can thus be cured,
future Onslows may.

NEIGHBORLY COURTESY.

HE following dogmatic correspondence will explain itself, and is therefore submitted to the public without further remark.

Letter from Mr. Manners to Mr. Beaston.

Sir, — It is now half-past seven on Monday morning, and your dog — he must be a large monster if he is as big as his voice — has been howling in the deepest double-bass ever since six o'clock on Saturday night. Probably he does not relish his tender out-door accommodations this inclement weather with nothing to lie on, and a blanket of the same for a coverlid. How would you like it, pray, if you were the dog and the dog were you, for a little space of thirty-seven hours and a half, the most of it made up of frost and tempest? Do you ever think of that when you push your poor beast out-of-doors, while it is raining knives and forks, but nothing for him, however, to eat with them? All dogs have their day, but yours has the night, too ; yet never a bone big enough to stop his mouth, as the neighbors can testify, for a single minute during the last thirty-seven mortal hours.

You have neighbors, you see, to consider, as well as a dumb brute, subjected to your caprice. They have ears yet, though they begin to suspect you must somehow have lost your own; for it seems impossible that any man would willingly suffer such a nuisance himself, however capable he may be of inflicting it on others. Where have you been living for the last day and two nights? If you have not gone to the dogs yourself, but are actually in the land of the living, your ears at least must certainly be dead, or past all surgery.

Under this supposition the neighbors have got me to let you know categorically, that when they close their doors and shutters at night they wish to shut up their ears also, and do not want you or any dog to open them again. In the daytime, also, they have a desire to reserve them for the music or conversation of their friends, and wholly object to having them filled by the ugly noises coming from your premises. You might as well thrust an entire dogwood-tree into our ears, and done with it, as to stuff them full of the bark. Deaf as you have proved yourself to be, we trust you will nevertheless listen to this remonstrance. If you fail us here, we shall try to reach you through some of your other senses.   Your injured neighbor,

G. MANNERS.

The next day, the following answer was returned from

Mr. Beaston to Mr. Manners.

Angry Sir, — I have received your snappish note about the dog, and cannot say I blame you much, though you seem deficient in philosophy. Your fault, however, may be that of being a young man, or rather green in city ways. So there is hope for you ; you will learn. The beauty of society is, that each man does what is right in his own eyes, and I may add, ears likewise. Some keep cats ; my next neighbor cherishes a crazy woman, who makes the welkin. ring, when she is in her paroxysms. Another entertains the public with the vocalism of a parrot ; while you sport a piano, and I believe occasionally a trombone ; and the gentleman just beyond certainly has a bugle and accordion. Now, I prefer the genuine bow-wow to any of the other nuisances ; and so I keep Bose chained in the yard to drown them. When he is visiting elsewhere, I stop my ears with cotton. This last specific I recommend to you ; it can ward off many social as well as political evils. Are you answered ?

Why, you will find that assaults upon the ear are not the worst. Somebody will establish a pig-sty, or a stable against your fence, looking right into your back-parlor, or open a currier's shop on one side of your front-door, a shed for shoeing horses

on the other, and a house or two for getting a genteel and easy, but not over-virtuous livelihood,
directly in front. You must not think of turning
up your pure and classic nose at these impurities,
but defend yourself by another, and learn to take
snuff without delay. Filthy streets, cesspools, leaky
gas-pipes, slaughter-houses, and reeking pot-houses,
you may then pass without annoyance. If any one
thinks that deadening the sensibility to evil does
not remove it, I have nothing to say; I am not a
reformer, but only a man of the world, who seeks
to shirk what he does not know how, and is unwilling, if he did, to take the trouble, to remedy.

If you live long, — I know you must be a youth,
— you will do as I do: let every one do as he likes,
and take care to get out of the way. If any fellow
fires balls out of an air-gun for amusement in the
streets, you must dodge. Take it for granted that
just as you attempt to cross a thoroughfare, the
driver of a cart will give his horse a chirrup and a
cut in order to run over you, or spatter you with
mud. If you see a load of calves piled up three
feet high in a wagon, with their heads dangling
over the raves against the wheels, or a lot of sheep
with their four legs tied into one, and thrown into
a burning sun, or on the frozen or snowy ground for
hours, it is no concern of yours; it is the way. All
you have to do is to wink, and these cruelties dis-

appear in a moment. That is what eyelids are given for. The old law maxim, when translated, has it, " Not to appear is the same as not to exist." For this reason it is no sort of matter that the cattle and sheep sold weekly in the New York market have nothing to eat for several days previous to being slaughtered, and consequently come near dying of starvation. Few know the fact, and so it is of no consequence in the least. As I despair of getting back to my dog again after wandering so far, I believe you must take this for an answer from your very indifferent neighbor,   A Beaston.

The reply to this letter has not come to hand; but it is easy to be seen there must have been one, because a disinfecting agent for social vices is a very different thing from one that only palliates, covers them up, or ignores them. An individual has no right to defend himself against one nuisance by making another equally outrageous. He that keeps a cur is said to be exposed to be first bitten if he should happen to go mad ; so he who unfeelingly inflicts discomfort on a neighbor will probably suffer for it as much himself in the end. The wretch who is deaf to the cries of a dog, or is capable of abusing a horse or sheep, cannot possess the feelings of humanity for a fellow-creature, much less any genuine Christian philanthropy. If we were to express our real sentiments with respect to Mr. Beaston and such as he, we should be apt to say that it would be no more than justice and perhaps to the advantage of both, if he and his dog were occasionally to change places. There is nothing like actual experience to impress instruction.

QUIDDLING.

E once knew a gentleman whose favorite interrogatory phrase was, "How goes the enemy?" meaning time. And in fact, that precious friend of man is treated as if he were the worst of enemies, to be abused, killed, got rid of in some way, by some artifice or deception. Among the ingenious contrivances to this effect, one of the most successful hitherto discovered is undoubtedly that known by the name of QUIDDLING. If " Procrastination is the thief of Time," Quiddling is its assassin. Where a man only puts off the performance of something an hour or a day, there is still an opportunity left to do some other act in the mean while. He may be said to treat time politely, as an acquaintance or a companion, according to the world's fashion, which exacts only the semblance, not the substance of a benefaction. But the Quiddler cannot, by anybody's ethics, be taken for a friend of time. He kills him. For, while madam or sir is annihilating the golden moments by a destructive mixture of worthless alloy,

they cannot, like the procrastinator, be doing anything else.

And what is quiddling, pray? " I don't remember," says one, " to have heard it enumerated
among the mortal sins, as you make it when you
charge the offender to be guilty of murder." We
will tell you what it is. It is spending five minutes
in doing a thing "just so," when the variation of a
hair's-breadth would make no difference. It is wasting a quarter of an hour before the glass to adjust a
curl, or give a graceful turn or color to a mustache.
It is the consumption of a whole forenoon to dress
for a walk, or of an entire afternoon to get ready
for an evening party. This consumption of time
can boast of more victims than the more talked-of
one of the lungs. He who is forever getting ready
to do something, and never does it, is a quiddler.
Life, as some live it, is an enormous preface to a
meagre work not finished, sometimes not begun.

If this matter were viewed as seriously as it
ought, there might be as pathetic a song written on
quiddle, quiddle, quiddle, as on "work, work, work."
A poor laborer is waiting for his breakfast; how
lamentably the good housewife spins round and
round, cutting all manner of figures, but not cutting
up the bread, nor ham. Here is a pretty fellow
who takes a quarter of an hour to tie his cravat, a
quarter to put on his coat, double that time to brush

his hair, pull on his gloves, and so on. If he has a letter to despatch, he is so tedious in selecting the paper and pen, and so shockingly nice and prosy in its composition, and so curiously particular and slow in affixing an appropriate, but ten to one a mistaken and fantastic seal, that the mail starts off without it.

This habit is very costly in more ways than one. None, therefore, but rich people can afford to be quiddlers. It is a luxury which, like the dyspepsia and gout, poor folks must not think of enjoying, any more than the privilege of lying abed till nine or ten, then toying an hour, as some hygienists recommend, over breakfast, two hours over dinner, another over a third, and perhaps a fourth meal ; thus reducing the definition of a human being to one who spends all his time in eating, sleeping, and dressing, and the remainder in drinking.

It is a sad misfortune to an author, or an artist, if the spirit of quiddling once insinuates itself. We cannot stop to relate its mischiefs, nor how it injured Akenside's " Pleasures of the Imagination," and drove Allston to paint half a dozen " Belshazzar's Feasts " one over the other, some worse and some better than the fragment finally left; which was made the fragment it is by quiddling.

If husband and wife are sinners in this respect alike, time ambles smoothly enough ; but to no purpose. If one alone is guilty, the yoke is carried unevenly, and trouble ensues. It has been said already, that quiddling is an expensive pleasure. One instance must suffice, and conclude this dissertation. A few weeks ago the following scene occurred : " Are you coming, my dear ? I shall be late." " Yes, husband, I shall be ready in a minute. I have only my hat to put on." That was true ; it had been equally true for full twenty minutes since she began to do it. Again the husband, " Come, come, wife, really I must go." " Almost ready," blandly replied the lady in the quietest tones. " Jeanette, positively I 'll go, can't stop another second," and the front-door was heard to open, before which the carriage had been waiting five-and-forty minutes, during most of which time the lady had been hard at work in drawing on her gloves and adjusting her bonnet, for all the rest of her rig was completed before. On hearing the opening of the door, she was aware the case was pressing, so began to move down-stairs gently, looking extremely nice, but not so tasteful in some of her arrangements as they were thirty minutes before she had altered them for the worse. At length they were off, and arrived in Wall Street just in time for the husband to learn that the subscription-books for a certain stock, which we shall not mention, had been closed, pursuant to previous notice, just six minutes and a half. Yesterday, he might have sold the shares reserved for him to the last moment at two thousand dollars advance. A costly hat, and an expensive wearer of it! But the wealthy have indulgences that others know not of, " and don't want to," somebody, looking over my shoulder, says.

THE UNKNOWN MAN.

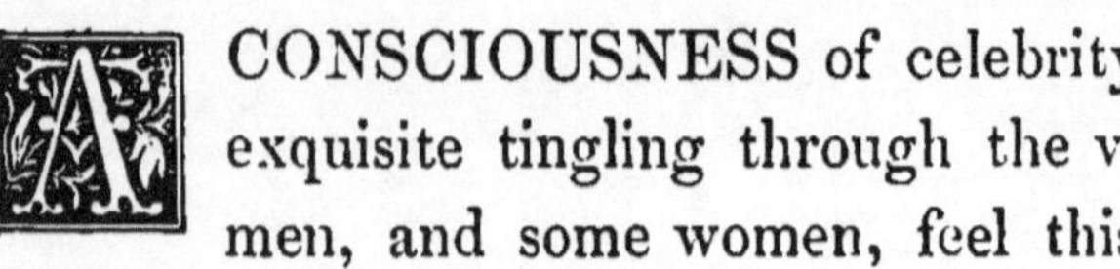

CONSCIOUSNESS of celebrity sends an exquisite tingling through the veins. All men, and some women, feel this delicious fever of the pulse. The thirst for fame, even of the lowest grades, is so intense in many as to make them totally unscrupulous about its quality, or their title to it. To them a counterfeit is just as good as any, provided it will pass. If they can get the credit, no matter for the substance. Reputation is everything, desert nothing. Still worse; bad fame to them is better than none at all, and to be cursed by every lip is preferable to not being mentioned at all.

But the delight of living *unknown* is not so generally admitted. Still it has some advantages. A young traveller in Europe enjoys the sweet immunity of secrecy among thronging millions. The espionage of home weighs no longer on the freedom of his heart. No eye of recognition is turned towards him. There is no one to dart the glance that checks the spontaneous wish, as it is bursting into action, or hush back into silence the half articulated word. The apprehension of the possible presence of an observer ceases; and the muscles of conformity, caution, and hypocrisy, enjoy at last a holiday, and, relaxed and idle, fall asleep, for want of provocation. Such perfect isolation is delightful, but quite impracticable where the most distant suspicion lurks that one acquaintance can possibly intrude.

Having made by travel this valuable discovery, the next thing is to render the beatitude perpetual. This will, indeed, appear almost a duty, on considering the sharp thorns which a love of distinction has planted in the breast, and the terrible crops of evil they have produced to wound it. If this briery harvest could only be removed from men's paths, what a glorious thing it would be to live ! We should walk then perpetually on roses. The history of man would be cut down from its thousand volumes folio to a single one no bigger than the " Pilgrim's Progress." Much gall and sulphate of iron would be saved, and rags, decaying and dropping off as now from paupers' backs, where they have been doing good service, would not undergo a resurrection in millions of books, where they are working mischief. Authors would then be happy in solitary contemplation on their immense geniuses, and try *to be* what they have *fancied* and described. If the race of Unknown men and women should chance to multiply to much extent, the importation of French frippery would fall off sadly, and opera-boxes become what booths are after Vanity Fair is over.

What a world of trouble does the Unknown Man escape! Nobody plagues him for his autograph, or certificates of the merits of cough-candy. No impertinent fellow sends him a letter telling him that he is a scoundrel or traitor to his country, obliging him at the same time to pay double postage for the information. The Unknown Man, secure in his panoply of nothingness, defies the cut of an impudent coxcomb of either sex, if such a creature can maintain a claim to any sex at all. Besides a material economy in hats, the multitude of fibs and maudlin compliments he shuns from not encountering a lady acquaintance is perfectly prodigious. Never invited to public dinners, he is entirely guiltless of the silly speeches delivered there, or of farcical letters apologizing for an absence that was expected and counted on. His name is not found upon electoral and jury lists, and so he is not pestered about his vote, nor fined for not spending a week in settling the difficulties of other people, when it has been the study of his lifetime to avoid any of his own. Quack and humbug handbills, which penetrate everywhere, like bad news and odors, fail to reach him, for his name cannot fortunately be discovered in the directory. Nobody asks him to head a subscription for getting Emerson's Essays translated into the English tongue, nor to sign a petition for the abolition of the potato rot on one side of thirty-six and a half degrees, or the social rot upon the other.

Having no reputation, he is not compelled, like authors and single ladies who are troubled with a surplus, to prosecute perpetually for slander to preserve it. He snaps his fingers at Mrs. Candor and Mrs. Charity, whose powers he thinks very highly of, but who cannot, let them do their best, by any kind of whispering, backbiting, or innuendo, make out to take away a character which one never had. There is, therefore, great comfort in being little. Such a man may cock his hat, and set the world at defiance ; for the police can no more take hold of him than of a jug without a handle.

He is not obliged to buy a pew in the broad-aisle of the distinguished Dr. ———'s church, or go to any one on Sunday, if he does not wish to, any more than the reverend clergy do themselves, when on their periodic European travels for their health,—an article which a thorough experience on their part has discovered to be best obtained where beauty, wealth, refinement, and the fine arts most abound.

He can speak of Clay, Calhoun, and Webster without fear of party whippers-in. If he chooses, he may, without loss of caste, decline to cover one of his extremities with French boots, or line the other with European affectation ; and can enjoy the privilege of using the old, blunt, honest Saxon style and manners, without first running them through a Gallic strainer. Being nobody, of course he can send an answer to a bore " that he is not at home," without a lie. Not the least of his good fortune is that of not being forced to dance with a rich dowdy, nor invited to indorse a speculator's note to the bank. No pickpocket asks him to be his bail, and the honor of suffering as surety for a political defaulter is denied him.

Invulnerable being ! He passes among man-traps thickly set by the artful sex, and yet comes away unhurt; for it takes the weight of gold to spring them. How happy ! He has only to write a successful tragedy, and he becomes at once the " Great Unknown," and enjoys the secret mightily. Should he happen to be hanged at last, he will pass mysteriously away, like the Man in the Iron Mask, and his relations will be forever spared any uncomfortable sensation about the throat, whenever hemp happens to be mentioned. When he dies he will take his name along with him, of course. In this he differs from the *would be* great and little immortals, who leave *theirs* behind to be kicked about a little while, and then sent after them.

The gentleman I have been describing received the other day the following epistle. I ought to add that he made immediately the acquaintance of the honest writer.

" Sir, — I have been your next-door neighbor for the last five years, and must do you the justice to acknowledge that I have never heard your name once mentioned nor yourself in any way alluded to in all that time. This is, therefore, necessarily addressed to you as No. 196. I suppose that I ought to ask forgiveness for recognizing your existence even now; but I promise not to do it again as long as I live, should you continue as deserving of obscurity as at present. But it was impossible wholly to withhold the credit due you for being so shining an example of a purely negative quantity, hitherto imagined, indeed, by mathematicians, but not actually exemplified before. Your position is certainly a happy one, since you can cut a figure without exciting envy, because that figure is a cipher. Your name, in consequence, has fortunately not been mixed up in the newspapers with those of pill-makers, pickpockets, great criminals, little politicians, philanthropists on a small scale, defaulters on a large one, and all the quacks, hacks, and dealers in everlasting clacks about blacks, to which may be added, by way of postscript, distinguished actors on the stage, and unpitied sufferers in pits and boxes, inventors of fancy shirts for those who can buy them, and verbose preachers of patience and endurance to those who cannot, but are obliged by poverty to make shifts for themselves.

"With sincere congratulations on your insignificance, I am, Sir, your unknown correspondent, and intend always to remain so,

"Frank Freespeech."

JESTS AND JESTING.

ESTS, notwithstanding their name, are very serious things, we assure you ; though they are trifles light as air, their manufacture is no joke, we are told. They must be thrown off, like French dancing, with a smile, and an air of ease and grace, though their original birth must without doubt have its severe labor-pains. We say original, because there are second-hand dealers in them, as well as in old clothes ; there are smiling, oily chapmen, and profiters by other people's toil.

Be so good as to turn your mind to the subject, and reflect what a jest really is. Like Dean Swift's leg of mutton, it must comprise the essence of many excellent things in philosophy and life, — the fruit of a happy faculty, improved by experience and study. Think not that the sudden flash that startles you is manufactured out of nothing. It comes from invisible, accumulated treasures, like the lightning which seems without either effect or cause in the summer evening sky. However much a *bon-mot* may cost the thinking faculty to invent, it must

come to the listener's ear with the same apparent
ease as sunshine to his eye, without a visible effort
from any quarter. Tom Moore, being complimented on the extreme facility as well as felicity of
composition apparent in his verses, answered: those
few lines you praise so much as having dropped
from the pen with as little effort as an apple from a
tree, when it is ripe, cost me days to mould into
their present shape.

Such is one class of jests; and they may well
enough be styled Sheridan jests, to commemorate
the way in which that eminent wit was in the habit
of preparing his admirable *impromptus.* There is,
however, another kind of the same genus, which
really come and go, like the old woman's soap, in a
manner not to be accounted for. The brains where
they are engendered need to be jostled, though ever
so little, and presto! out issues a *jeu d'esprit,* such
a kaleidoscope of ideas! They are really agreeable
and striking, but obey no known laws. Such a
brain possesses an infinite variety of modifications,
but is not master of its own creations. They are
merely born to it, not made by it ; they come, and
the thing that comes is a come-by-chance. Consequently, the owner of such an occiput is not
fairly an accountable being, — in the matter of his
jokes, we mean. He cannot help them. He does
not set his brain in motion; it moves itself, and

therefore is frequently out of proper tune and season. Such a fellow conceives jests at a funeral of a friend, almost as freely as at a marriage or the club-room. Sometimes he gives them utterance without a thought : he regrets and is ashamed of it ; but there they are, and he cannot always help it.

This natural jester consequently makes enemies, — more than the Sheridan wit, because his ebullitions are not under his control. Being as little under his control as a spirited horse, his spontaneous wit runs away with his rider frequently, and does much mischief, for which in reality he ought to be no more accountable than Virgil's cows, who used to be fecundated at certain seasons with the West wind ; or Congress-water for its gas ; and not so much as a poor fellow whose head-piece has given way under a shower of grape-juice. For in the latter case, the man was the real author of his own fortune ; the other foible may be traced back to nature. That man was brought into this breathing world without his knowledge or consent, with a brain which could not help its comical combinations any more than the prism can on the other hand avoid its refraction of the component rays of light.

It is a common saying, that jests break no bones. That may be, but still do worse ; for they may, and frequently do, wound the feelings, and break the ties of friendship. A custom of jesting may gain the reputation of wit in society, but cause the loss of its respect. It has impeded and not unfrequently entirely prevented the success in life of the most brilliant intellects. Whether the habit of cracking jokes is looked upon as connected with breaking promises we do not know; but it seems to imply frailty of some sort, and volatility, which may run from the head to the habits, and contaminate the character by making it as unstable and fluctuating as the wit.

And now what would you have? You cry down a nimble playfulness of the fancy; would you have a young fellow as dull and serious always as an oyster, so that he may be the better liked? No, not so. He may be a buffo sometimes; but a buffoon never. He may show that he can be frolicksome, ingenious, and even fantastical in brain-work, if he pleases; yet he is never to forget that these must be exceptions from his general state of mind. The background of his character must be serious and reflecting. If a man is found to be ever cracking witticisms, the common inference, and a just one too, will be, that his brain is cracked to quite as great an extent as his jokes.

SUGAR AND VINEGAR IN MAN.

ROM thorough investigations the following conclusions have been gathered : That sugar is a normal product in man ; that it is secreted in the liver, and that this is a normal function of that organ. The source of its supply is from nitrogenized elements, and the food furnishes it to the system. All this we find in a medical work. We propose to add to it a fact not discovered by chemical anaylsis or microscopic examination, but by dint of experience, and observations of the naked eye, without glasses. The human system produces vinegar as well as sugar ; we might add gall too, but that is reserved for another occasion. Our attention is now restricted to the *acid* in human nature.

Persons enough may be found, no doubt, who are skeptical of the sweet said to be discovered in the liver, or elsewhere ; but we should like to see one who questions the fact that men's faces are frequently full of vinegar. Neither is that all ; for, notwithstanding the liver distils sugar, it cannot be denied that there are other organs where the acetous fermentation is constantly going on, from which any quantity of the best of vinegar — not the New York grocer's drug of that name — may be obtained. In truth, a man may be regarded as a huge vinegar-cruet, as well as a sugar-bowl. These two ingredients are laid up in his system to be used from time to time as flavor for actions and conversations.

These sweets and acids require only to be dexterously distributed to constitute a piquant character, and a not unpleasant companion. When intercourse becomes rather flat and stale, it imparts to it an agreeable relish and helps to wake up drowsy people, if a scruple or two of sharp acid be dropped into the dish of discourse. And so, when crab-sticks prevail inordinately in your club or association, to introduce a real sugar-cane of a man among them, full of the juice of love and kindness, has an admirable effect. We have known the experiment to work almost a miracle. Every one of the crabbed sticks, as if ashamed of himself, would try to appear as genial and melting as his saccharine brother. It was a failure, it is true ; but if they possessed not his rich flavor and fatness, their acidities were considerably mollified, which was a clear gain.

But it will not do to have too many vinegar-bottles in society.   It is to be feared they are already too numerous for the sugar-canes.   Under this impression, and apprehending that the disproportion is increasing, we have engaged some chemists, particularly those who are distinguishing themselves by doing so much to fertilize our soils and improve our candies, to try and see what discoveries can be effected in the human microcosm.   They have been especially enjoined to inquire, if other organs beside the liver do not yield sugar.   Our own opinion is, that the heart ought to be the most abundant producer of sugar in the whole organism.   And we are sure of one thing, which is, that however small or large the quantity might be from that pure source, the real value of it would far exceed that of all the other organs of the body put together.

16

<h1 style="text-align:center">THE PLAUSIBLE MAN.</h1>

THERE are downright persons, and what is better, there are also upright. Between these is still another class, the resultant of the two, who may be called diagonal men. When one hears of anybody, before unknown, he naturally desires for information how he dresses, how he looks. The diagonal man, being the resultant of the two forces, is of course a progress man; but it must be acknowledged, that, as is apt to be the case with such people, he is progressive in the direction of his own interests. But we must not forget to mention how you may know him, should you happen some day to meet him as you turn a corner.

His hair is inclined to lankness; very rarely, perhaps never, curls; for that property implies crispness, and a certain dryness, insinuating that the wearer himself may, from the attrition of his dry qualities, flash suddenly into a pun. This the *plausible* man, for your diagonal is very plausible, never does. He is too oily for that. We will not assert that the plausible man's hair is always oily, we must first ask Dr. Redfield, but we are certain that his tongue is. We will not give that up for Dr. Redfield, nor Mr. Fowler neither. His words are smooth and sweet, implying an extraordinary natural organ, which art, equal at least to that of a *prima donna*, has wonderfully improved, and constant practice kept well lubricated. One can never mistake that downcast, half sheepish, half foxy look; demure, yet expressing in very articulate dumb-show a conviction that his perfect disinterestedness and generosity are by no means understood. Yes, that is he. The plausible man dresses himself in the most studied and careful half-quakerish style possible, and then wonders he is not taken for the model of simplicity and naturalness that he pretends to be.

Thus does the plausible man look. We do not inquire what he does; for he does nothing; the man is made to talk; that is his mission (to use the *original* expression) in the world. He talks. Ye gods! how he can talk! There is no occasion that anybody else in the universe should ever say another word. When the plausible man opens his oily mouth, and begins to speak, " let no dog bark," and all creation beside be silent, and, like the Roman mimes, occupy themselves in making gestures to such an accomplished actor. No matter what the subject is, anything or nothing, he is equal to it; whether it is of a domestic nature, or turns on travel abroad, he is perfectly at home.

Plausible men shine everywhere, — even where other people generally look dull; in afflictive dispensations (of others) and at funerals. But if they have what are sometimes denominated strong points, these lie, perhaps, in their peculiar qualifications for Wall Street and Washington, — we mean for pecuniary and political science. Talk, glib and oily, everybody knows, is the motive power in both. There is, indeed, no substitute. This is a postulate.

Every financier and politician begins with it, as the grammarian with his alphabet. Though an incredibly active and persistent force which can never be superseded, still we do not claim it to be the actual secret of the veritable perpetual motion. Talk is only conditionally that power. We believe it would be kept up by these fair-seeming plausible men in financiering, and in congress, till their objects were accomplished, though the world might end first; but in real practice, such men always attain their objects, and so the wordy motion ends.

As to the designs of this class of individuals, for they always have them, and pretty well defined ones too. They are not generally the worst that might be mentioned. Such persons are not cruel. They wish neither to rob, nor murder, nor in fact to do anything by force. If they have any thirst for blood, the leech is a proper type for the propensity, and not the tiger. But in fact they do not desire the harm of any one whatever for the harm's sake, but only as a means of good to themselves. They entertain no ill-will against any of their brethren of the race ; on the contrary, they have a positive liking, if not for your person itself, at any rate for the property, power, or other advantage that belongs to it. While they are squeezing out of society and you all that is practicable, they wish you both well with what is left; and will sometimes, like the generous highwayman, or the equally generous Jenny Lind, make you a present of a small part of what they have taken from you. This last manœuvre is the highest manifestation of the plausible man.

The plausible man wishes well to all mankind ; especially to himself, as one of that great multitude whom he is best acquainted with, and particularly attached to. In accomplishing the object of benefiting himself, he finds from long and sage experience that the readiest way is, when thus engaged, to imitate the ventriloquist, and direct the notice of observers to a distant spot as the scene of action, while all his energies are in the mean while concentrated with preternatural intensity in his own person.

PLEASURE OF BEING A GRANDFATHER.

T does not belong to us to choose our lot in life ; if it did, that of the Grandfather should be ours. For just consider, if you please, what the term implies. It may conjure up in some minds, for aught we know, a rheumy-eyed old man, troubled with catarrh and cough, with shrunk shanks a world too narrow for his pantaloons, smelling strongly of tobacco and something worse perhaps, with everything dead within him but his impatient and choleric temper. This is one grandfather to be sure ; but there are two to every family, and it is the other one we mean. He is not a very old gentleman after all ; and might pass for a young one often, if he chose, without a discovery of the counterfeit, though there is a risk of being found out on trial, as our apparent 36's were in the war with England, as 74's in disguise.

But one of the pleasures of being a grandfather consists in his having been a son. He remembers when he was a rosy-faced, curly-headed boy, sliding on the ice, or sailing his tiny fleet of vessels in a gutter. Some can go farther back, and recollect how they used to climb upon the lap and shoulders of their beautiful mothers, and kiss them and their handsome young aunts with their lovely companions, by the score. The celebrated Fisher Ames, one of the most eloquent and amiable men of our country, who died about fifty years ago in Dedham, must have been able to recall scenes still more interesting, for he was not weaned from his mother till he was eleven, and he entered Harvard College in one year after. These are charming warm pictures to carry with one into the frosty January of old age, to play around the heart and fancy, when they have lost the capacities or relish for new enjoyments, and prefer old images to fresh realities. So, you see, the grandfather possesses a youthful world within him in addition to the outward one, as it appears through the medium of his failing vision.

But the grandfather has also had the pleasure of being a father. To qualify him for that relation, he has, or ought to have, felt the soul-subduing passion, which alone exemplifies the much talked of universal empire. Of course, he possessed, or thought he did, which is the same thing, a gem of beauty in his wife ; and if "a thing of beauty is a joy forever," then the grandfather is certainly not deficient in materials for comfort. The fatherly period is the time for activity, business, and accumulation, and we have heard it said that an individual enjoys the getting, more than the spending of his property. This may be true, so far as the identical individual is concerned. The question in our mind is, whether he enjoys the acquisition of money, better than his heir does its expenditure. If he does, all we have to say is, that a prosperous, money-getting father and his prodigal son are a couple of the very happiest fellows in Christendom. Whatever share of happiness, however, ought of right to be allotted to each of these relations, the grandfather, it is obvious, knows all about it, and must enjoy a lively recollection of both. By a kind of descent, which travels backward and upward, he may be said to inherit the pleasures of the father and the son by recollecting them. Thus, as the son is emphatically said to be the father of the man, they both together must of course be the grandfather of the same individual.

But the felicity of the grandfather is not all a thing of memory. A great deal of it is a fresh achievement of his old age. What! is there no delight in having half a dozen little funny-eyed grandchildren chasing the blue devils out of every room in the house with their sunny faces? Is it nothing to have some of them pulling at every limb of your body, beside an extra one swinging from your hair, or seeing whether there is not room for him in your pockets, or where the hole in your ear goes to? Surely the grandfather's hat and spectacles are becoming to that chubby fellow, who is so attentively reading the morning's newspaper, which the old gentleman has been looking for, a quarter of an hour in vain. What if he can't go out without his hat and cane, which one of the boys is playing horse with in the yard, nor stay at home without his spectacles and newspaper; is he not a happy man in being thus used up for the gratification of his offspring? We know it must be so; and that the sweets and satisfactions of life are extracted from its irregularities and odd humors, just as pearls are made out of the disorders in the oyster. Think of this, old bachelors, and believe that the plagues which others cause you are fruitful in good, from which if you are exempt, suicidal plagues will spring up within. Between these two there is as great a difference as having one's house warmed by the natural heat of the sun's rays or by setting its own furniture on fire.

The greatest drawback from the satisfaction of the grandfather must arise from the consciousness that it has not long to last. From what we have remarked of men advanced in life, we mean of old men who are also old gentlemen, we think with Cicero, that they possess more of the elements of contentment than persons at any other period of life. But there is a canker which mars all its quiet satisfaction, and that is, its instability. This was a knotty difficulty to surmount, if we remember rightly, by the philosophic Roman. But we can do now what was impossible in the age of Tully. If a good man and a Christian, the aged person may derive hope and comfort, not draw a gloomy apprehension, from the prospect of his dissolution. Such an event will improve his condition, not impair it, by introducing him to a sphere where advanced stages of excellence and felicity will exist, but where everything belonging to old age will be unknown.

OLD AGE.

AN aged man with silver hair, sitting at the root of a branching oak that had seen a hundred winters, and was now in the autumn shedding its century leaves, — this is a striking subject for the pencil, though we do not remember to have seen it painted. He is looking upward, while the foliage has fallen around to cherish and protect the young acorns, which are destined to perpetuate the race of the patriarch of the forest. But no canvas can set forth the thoughts and feelings of the old man, as he revolves in his mind the various fortunes, gales, soft breezes, fair weather and foul, that have wafted him hither, from his earliest boyhood. In the course of his long wanderings, he has taken deep draughts of pleasure and joy. He has also known full well the bitterness of misfortune in the deprivation of property, or the loss of some who were very dear, perhaps of both. And though when his blood ran hotly through his veins in the prime of manhood, he could enjoy keenly, yet never perhaps has he known a se-
rener and more perfect happiness than he feels at

this moment on the verge of the grave, among the fading foliage of the ancient oak.

Such a man, during his long pilgrimage, must have seen much sorrow; for every year, as it scores its passage on our foreheads, at the same time pours another drop of bitter into our enjoyments. Yet he was never less vulnerable to sorrow than now. As he descends into the vale of years, the light of common joys may become less bright, and his horizon may be diminished. But his spiritual vision becomes clearer. As he looks up through the naked branches of the old oak spreading over his head, and finds his sight unobstructed by the thick summer foliage that once shut out the sky from his view; now, in his old age, when his hair has grown thin, and his worldly honors have fallen around him, he can see in the open prospect the firmament of heaven glittering with inumerable hosts of celestial lights. What Ossian sung of the sun may be said of this ancient man, " The oaks of the mountains shall fall; the mountains themselves decay with years; the ocean shrink and grow again; the moon herself be lost in heaven; — but thou shalt be forever the same, rejoicing in the brightness of thy course. When the world shall be dark with tempests; when the thunder shall roll and lightning fly; thou shalt look in thy beauty from the clouds, and laugh at the storm."

TO MY MOTHER, ON HER ATTAINING THE AGE OF EIGHTY-EIGHT YEARS.

ALL day the traveller sees the mountain tower
Along his path, and still at evening's hour
    It cuts the distant sky;
The forest wild is past, the well-tilled plain,
The river, spire, and the abodes of men,
    Are sunk below his eye:

Yet still that dearly loved, familiar sight,
As fast around him falls the gathering night,
    His saddening bosom cheers;
Still brave Monadnock rears his changeless form,
Unmindful if the day shall shine or storm,
    Or close in smiles or tears.

And such, dear mother, have you been to me,
From even the earliest dawn of memory,
    Near sixty years agone;
In this long pilgrimage, unseen or seen,
The thought of you has my horizon been
    In airy circle drawn.

Who else but you can waken memory's power,
That links my age with childhood's transient hour,
    And brings again the boy?

This spell you can create for me, but who
Shall e'er the days of youth to you recall,
　　And echo back their joy?

Age is unlovely, yet in you how blest!
In tresses white and spotless virtue drest,
　　As winter's heaven-dropped snow;
Unsoiled, awhile it flings abroad its light,
Till, wasted and exhaled from mortal sight,
　　It shines no more below.

So on the verge of fourscore years and ten
You stand in thought serene and fix your ken
　　Upon a loftier sphere;
Where age, its journey done, its load thrown down,
Soars up to take its everlasting crown
　　Of joy without a tear.

CHESS.

OME time ago we found occasion to say
something on the " Tendencies of the Game
of Chess." The great interest felt in the
subject, and attention paid to it at present and for
the year past, which, owing to the triumphs of
Morphy in Europe, and his expected return to his
native country, will probably continue for some
time to come, justifies inquiry, not only into its
character as a liberal and elegant amusement, but
also into the claims which have been set up for it
as a powerful agent for augmenting and disciplining
the mental faculties. That it does this for the faculty of memory will be at once conceded. But
how far does this agency extend? This is the
present question.

It is a common remark, which Franklin may
have countenanced, that great practice and skill in
the movement of pieces in this fascinating game
conduce to the strengthening of the powers of reasoning, and of that faculty of combination which is
of such inestimable value to the commander of an

army. But we conceive there is no analogy in the two cases. The movement in Chess is of pieces of absolutely certain power; the force of every one, the pawn, bishop, knight, queen, and the rest, is definite, and perfectly settled. The adversaries in the game are also both equally well acquainted with the extent of their own force and that of each other. Nothing is hidden, or left to conjecture. But in war, how different is all this! The force which a general can move is of uncertain amount. It is still more doubtful how that of his antagonist compares with his own. Hence, it appears that a mathematical judgment, which is certain, can be exercised with respect to the forces of both parties in a game of Chess; but in war all is conjecture, and whatever reasoning there is upon those matters, namely, the forces and movements of corps and squadrons, is moral reasoning, whereas the reasoning about the forces and movements of all the pieces on the chess-board is strictly mathematical, since they are all given and defined, as much as angles and lines in geometry.

Then there are other facts which control, or largely affect, the fate of battles and war, that do not exist at all in the mimic Chess. These facts are not only the number and quality of the battalions, but their positions, both relatively to each other and to the enemy; the time required to bring them up and move them into action. These and similar points are all settled in Chess. Then there is the exceedingly important but never to be anticipated fact, how the men will behave in battle. Will some timidity, or more or less hesitation affect them? Will they do better or worse than formerly? or, if new recruits, then comes the doubt how far they are to be relied on. After all, how much depends on the prestige of a commander, who has been in a hundred battles and never once defeated! A Napoleon in the immediate command would be all but invincible; the sight of him, the knowledge that he was among them, would double the strength and efforts of an army, and would be felt like an arrival of a fresh reinforcement wherever he might be.

All these circumstances, and similar ones, are to be calculated by a skilful general, and the accuracy of this judgment constitutes his greatness. It is obvious, we need not say, that none of them, though so essential with respect to the fate of a battle, exist at all in the Chess contest. In this there is no room for moral calculation. All is arithmetical, and no faculties but those of memory and computation have any place. Most or all of the problems with which the general has to struggle, overcome, or avoid, some of which have been mentioned, are wholly unknown to the Chess-player. We may add to those which have been already alluded to, his plans for subsisting his troops, the difficulties his opponent is likely to encounter in this respect, the geographical nature of the locality where a battle is to be brought on, the sudden and quick changes of the programme of the battle. The *time* in which operations are performed in war is of the last importance. In Chess, as every one knows, a player may take one minute or twenty to make his move in. If that amount of precious time were lost in battle, it is easy to see that the consequence would be fatal.

In short, whatever foresight of a certain sort may be taught by Chess, it is clear that it is of a very different nature from that required by a general; and its logic is not the logic of a lawyer, orator, nor statesman, but resembles most that of the geometer. But generals, philosophers, and moral reasoners are not made great or greater by uncommon skill in the game of Chess.

THE SPEECH-MAKER.

D O you see that man just getting into the stage ? Aye. Very well, then you are looking on one who has made a speech in public. Why, you don't say so; really, and he has actually made a speech, has he ? How many, pray ? Only one. That is odd. To make a speech is a great affair, it is true; but to stop there, and attempt no more, as things go, is little less than miraculous. It requires only a tongue, which most people have, to be able to talk in private or in public either, — and he who can do one tolerably, can do the other also, — but to be silent shows brains, a higher organ than the tongue. Consider what a restless thing the latter is, never quiet; hung, as some affirm, in the middle; tempted to action, like the magnetic needle, by a thousand disturbing forces. Truly, to make a speech is great; but to do it only once is greater still. It immortalized the English Hamilton, surnamed the Single-Speeched, and deservedly. For when was it ever known that a man who had delivered even a bad speech ever

failed to try again and again? and we have known
more than one keep on trying till they were three-
score years and ten, with indifferent success.

I will not take it upon me to say that the gentleman who has taken his seat yonder will rest content
with his one short effort. Oh, it was short, was it?
Then be assured it will not be long before you get
another from him. In the mean time, I hope he
will excuse me for staring a little at such a phenomenon as a single-speech gentleman. Have you
not observed, that your public talker will never
give up his privilege of boring the community till
he has shown his ability to manufacture a long
speech? It is a lamentable fact. But that is not
the worst of the discovery he thus makes. Having
found out that he can go on uttering the hundred
thousand words of the language as long as they
will hold out and he can stand upon his legs, a
new desire springs up within him to gratify this
ambition. Taciturnity will not do, as once; that
ice has been broken long ago, and never can be
mended. But, alas! a speech of ordinary length
will never serve his purpose now. He goes stren-
uously for length, with little regard to the other
dimensions. The day of his shortcomings — no sin
in him — is unfortunately over, and he has evidently
embarked in the enterprise of discovering the longitude in language.

Speech-making is the art of putting one's thoughts into as many words as possible. The Hebrew lexicon which we studied in our college-days was a very thin octavo volume, not equalling the dignity of a respectable monthly, or even pamphlet, of these times. Yet it contained the elements of those inspired, sublime, and tender lyrics of the King of Israel, and other poets of that country, which have roused the devotion and soothed the sorrows of all enlightened people since their time, for thirty centuries. This book contained but a few hundred words; the last edition of Webster's dictionary numbers nearly one hundred thousand! What an everlasting thread of sentences cannot a language-spinner manufacture out of these? It requires a mechanical, not a mental talent. Given, a quantity of words, how much space can they be made to cover? That is the question with the speechifier; just as with the goldsmith, how much wooden timber can be gilded with a minute lump of gold. Homœopathy has invaded more regions than that of physic. The inquiry is heard everywhere, how far the most insignificant means may be made to answer? to what possible extent a limited quantity of ideas and provisions can be made to suffice in a speech or boarding-house? Carlyle deemed the clothing of the physical man an ample and proper subject to write a book about. The art of cutting out and making up the drapery of thought, so that a man may appear to be somebody, when he is really only a column of more or less good words, deserves therefore to be cultivated, as it is, by thousands. It is a worthy and lucrative trade, and is one of our home-manufactures, which is more encouraged than almost any other. Hollow ware and books, with as little in them as the ware, can be imported sufficient to satisfy the public wants. So, indeed, speeches may be, and are. But dinner-speeches are thought not so good, when cold, and therefore must have their sauce, if not their substance, prepared at the time of consumption, or a little before ; sometimes a little after, according to report.

It is on the occasions just hinted at, when wine and words, not always wit, begin to flow, that young beginners love to make their first essays in oratory, which sometimes end like the first flights of new-fledged birds from the nest — by coming to the ground. But in both cases they fall upon the tender bosom of mother earth, or that of friends made more forbearing and good-natured by generous wine. Thus the first degree in verbiology is taken in this school, when every one is so full of good eating, drinking, and good-nature, as to have no room for anything but song and sound. Words strung together, and jingling like bells upon the tongue, are almost as certain of approbation as " the bones " and the banjo.

From this cradle of the art of speaking it is only a step upon a level to the caucus hall. Here, the same love of music, with or without words, encourages the rhetorical apprentice. Have you never observed how exceedingly common is the narrative or story-telling faculty? Many of the class have small heads. An old adage runs thus, —

> " Great head and little wit;
> Little head and not a bit."

Thus assigning the highest powers of intellect to heads of the ordinary size. Is this so? We do not decide the point, because a year ago people were measuring skulls, and ascribing most intellect to Cuvier, Webster, Dupuytren, and others, till somebody got hold of the skull of a blockhead that was big enough to contain more brains than any of them. However that may be, it has been remarked that little heads and great talkers go together. We have known more than one such who could talk all day, it cannot be said without exhaustion, but without cessation. Such a person finally stops, but one cannot see why. Words are not wanting; all in the dictionary may have been employed; but they can be used to as good purpose again. Of ideas, properly belonging to the speaker, there were few or none at first, and so the scarcity of them is not minded. The talking power is, in fact, a low faculty, as may be observed in Congress, and has not been conspicuous in the highest order of intellects. It is largely recollective, and found most in persons not original in their conceptions, but turning spontaneously for nourishment to other fountains not within themselves.

But look! our one-speech gentleman is about to ruin his distinctive reputation. He is getting out of the stage and actually going into —— Hall, where they hold political assemblies. That honorable surname will be no longer his; he will be degraded to the level of the chattering crew, who fancy they discover talent by an ordinary display of one of the vulgar capacities of the race.

SIC UTERE TUO, UT ALIENUM NON LÆDAS. — THE ACCORDION.

O use one's own rights and property so as not to injure those of another, is a dictate of natural justice, a prompting of common politeness, and a commandment of Christianity. Nobody doubts the law, or its universal obligation; the difficulty is to regulate its multifarious applications. A man has an unquestionable natural right to extend his arm to the utmost of its length, and with all the vigor he is master of; but if he does it in a crowd, and happens to knock a fellow-creature down, he is liable for assault and battery. There is no trouble at all in deciding on such a case; a man need not read law three years first.

If anybody should undertake to stick the person of another full of pins, especially that portion of it denominated the ears, without his consent first had and obtained, what would a large majority of people think of the proceeding? Probably as decidedly objectionable and unneighborly. The general sentiment would be opposed to turning any individual,

however soft, into a pin-cushion. We will then put a
pin in there, and go to the next case, which may
admit a question in the minds of some.

If an innocent gentleman, or lady, has taken it
into his head or hand to learn to play that very
manly, genteel, and expressive instrument, the accordion — ah ! the old imp always comes at the mention
of his name; we hear its sickening dulcet voice
this very minute, repeating all the nigger-melodies
that the universe has been nauseated with for the
last five years. It is impossible for us to go on till
that horrid accordion stops, which will not happen
till bedtime, unless somebody calls and — thank
heaven ! the bell rings, and the bellows-blower is
summoned into the house from the piazza, where he
nightly robs the neighborhood of quiet, and persists
in occupying their unwilling ears with just such
noises as he chooses to inflict upon them. This man
arrogates the right of dictating to the whole vicinity
what and how they shall enjoy, or rather what they
shall suffer, every evening of the warm season of the
year. Why, one would suppose that none but a
dog or cat would continue obstinately to bark and
yell contrary to the wishes of all their hearers.
This practice cannot be properly called murder, we
suppose, though it is making an end of our happiness and peace. If it is not homicide, it is certainly
every other offence known to any code. It is petty

larceny, for it steals away our precious quiet, — grand larceny, in depriving us of it for a whole evening. Was there ever, too, a plainer case of assault and battery, as well as trespass *quare clausum*, than this wanton invasion of our castle, in its sleeping chambers, and cruelly wounding the ears of its inhabitants?

What possible justification can there be for this enormous breach of the peace? Unwilling to impute it to the depravity of the human heart, we are obliged to set it down, of course, to some imperfection in the head. The offending party must be too musical, that is, possess too much ear. A superfluity of ear is certainly a misfortune to any creature. But that circumstance can be no justification for the infliction of its braying upon other persons, with a total disregard of consequences.

It is not pleasant, we admit, in order to exempt such offenders from criminality, thus to charge them with stupidity. But how can it possibly be helped? If it were the case of a tobacco consumer, simply puffing a quantity of nasty smoke into one's face ; or of a regular eater of the vermin-killing weed, gently depositing his saliva on your coat-tail ; or of a sweet girl, gracefully shaking a foot-rug from a window precisely over your head, on passing by a house, or, as you are carefully tiptoeing along, sweeping the dirt of the steps plump into your breeches-pocket, at the same time that a lady, who is meeting you, pokes her umbrella into your right eye ; if it were any, or all of these, and scores besides that might be mentioned, not a word should be lisped in opposition.   To such petty annoyances we are all accustomed.   They are supposed, like the monopoly of all the best seats at a public table, and what is of more consequence, all the nice bits on it, to be inseparably connected, somehow or other, as Southern slavery is, with American liberty.   They are therefore borne with pleasure, as people tolerate puppies and poor relations, on account of their belonging to a rich lady, or influential family.

But when any individual, male or female, presumes to fill our aching ears with sounds of his own making, and persists in the outrage by the hour together, — ears perhaps consecrated by the voice, the better part, of the divine Jenny Lind, and still vibrating with the precious sounds which she has manufactured expressly for their use at a very high price,—the impudence of the transaction is absolutely astounding.   Indeed, the confidence of musicians is frequently amazing ; but the ignorant self-esteem, in particular, of this nocturnal disturber of repose and comfort through the medium of the accordion — we hate all mediums — can never be adequately described.   One thing we would leave on record, as the conclusion of the matter.   Let no one make the

silly mistake of thinking that other persons will admire his music, conversation, or appearance, quite as
much as he does himself.   Depend upon it, nobody
loves any noise long, that is not of his own making ;
and every man, if his smelling-organ must be pulled,
prefers to have it done with his own particular thumb
and finger.

THERE'S LIGHT IN THE TOMB.

A SONNET.

WITH pleasure once I thought of death; I sighed
To close my weary eyes in sleep profound
Upon the pleasant world, that smiled around,
And fly to where the lost from earth abide.
'T was not Ambition's promises denied,
Subduing sickness, poverty, nor pain,
Which thus in me triumphantly defied
The gloomy horrors of the grave's domain.
I saw them not, or, if I did, they were
Like ancient ruins that in moonlight lie,
Illumed with beauty by the bright and fair,
Who passed along them to their native sky:
Ah! that this momentary dream might last,
Nor be dissolved, till life is overpast.

A SONNET.

GREAT Missionary to the human heart,
That spirit-world, where heathen gods abound,
Alike on Christian and on Paynim ground,
The Gospel to this mighty waste impart.
'T is thine to scan the soul, its joy and smart,
See glimpses of the Infinite Profound,
O'erwhelmed by brutish appetite around,
And back to heaven lead man's immortal part.
No need the tropics fiery sands to roam ;
Lo! pagans live before thy eyes at home.
To these dark " spirits in prison,'' it is thine
To speak on themes, O Dewey, which shall fill
Celestial natures, and with rapture thrill,
When burning constellations cease to shine.

THE PASTOR.

HERE is an office that requires in the incumbent the head of Socrates and heart of John.

The great are too great for it; yet it is larger than the ability of any who ever held it.

An emperor, in the interval of his insane ambition, sighed for the peace and happiness of its lot.

Demanding the strength of an angel, what fools have not rushed in to seize upon its vestments?

Fanaticism feels no fervor that may not at some time become a pastor of a Christian flock; prudence possesses not too much caution for his perpetual control.

A pastor is not the handiwork of good or wicked men in lawn sleeves; he is the child of God; not made, but born.

Many have desired to wear the crown of Jesus, but divested of its thorns.

Yet some have had the courage to crucify the flesh; for which a portion of them have sought a compensation in the increase of their pride.

There are those who would willingly uphold the crosier, but have not the strength ; a fit trust for a babe in Christ, it nevertheless asks the power of a man, and the meekness of a disciple.

He who seeks it for its honors, shall not find them. The fame of a good man, striving to approach the Sun of righteousness, is a shadow, which falls behind him, and he regards it not.

Thousands have occupied the pastoral office ; few have filled it. Humility it asks for, not weakness ; the unction of the inner life, fountain of external courtesy ; yet a Christian, rather than a gentleman. It was not found too narrow for the soul of Jesus ; it sometimes dwindles to the dimensions of a child.

Will a man not tremble to seek a living, merely, in a priesthood within the bosom of which his Master died ?

Learning in its incumbent is not to be contemned ; but it becomes a noxious parasite, if suffered to exhaust the oil destined also for the nourishment of the affections, or to overshadow the tender vines of the spirit.

Let no one complain that a greater burden is laid upon him than he is able to bear ; it is better that the citadel should be unwatched, than that the warder should be faithless to his post.

What wretchedness is like his who is travelling away from his affections ; whose life hangs a millstone on every word which he utters in the sanctuary!

Before he receives the Great Commission, the young Evangelist reads upon it the triumphs of the Cross, and feels the spirit of a martyr; after it is given him, he finds, recorded on the other side, its sufferings and persecutions; then he feels the martyrdom of his spirit.

Is a son of the Church preëminent for administrative talents? It is a good gift; yet let him often remember who it was that carried the bag.

Pulpits create a great gulf; yet sermons have their use. Abraham did well in preaching to the Rich Man; but the disciples long to be taken, like Lazarus, to the preacher's bosom. The Saviour of the world taught much, but loved more. He was the companion of men and women, and took their little ones in his arms.

The Church of Christ requires not a government; but government stands in need of the Christian Church. One secularizes the clergy; the other sanctifies the laity.

Modesty of manners and opinion in a young minister are winning to the heart, like unconsciousness of beauty in a maiden; there are no arrows so resistless as those which are feathered with the bashfulness of such a one.

Heads grow weary of giving and receiving intellectual blows; but the loving heart, though ever pouring out its streams, is never empty, and the sympathizing bosom is never tired of imbibing them, yet is not full.

A minister may neither be a Griffin nor a Channing; still, if he possesses a true heart, he will not be in danger of fatiguing his flock. An affectionate speech has no commonplaces.

The good pastor receives us when infants to his arms, and washes us with the emblematic water of regeneration; at our maturity, he ratifies on earth our matrimonial vows, first registered in heaven; stands by our bedside in the final struggle; and shines, like the sun within the Arctic circle, upon bereaved ones at the midnight of their sorrows.

Such a servant of the Cross have I known; such were ——, and ——; but I will not name them. I will not ask the world to remember those who can never be forgotten.

DARK CHURCHES.

A CHURCH is a place for light, its distribution, its reception. Yet it has grown to be one of the darkest spots ever visited, every ray of sunshine being carefully excluded. In New York there is more than one of these wells of obscurity, where the worshippers stumble in the aisles, if not " on the dark mountains," because some trustee, minister, or sexton, or other, has read of the Cathedral's " dim, religious light." In fact, we know a man as well as we do ourself, who has not seen his own minister, while in the pulpit, for ten years past, though he generally goes to church twice every Sunday. He has learnt to tell him, as well as all strange preachers, by their voices.

But it is gratifying to see, as well as hear, an individual who is talking to you, if persuasion to right living is the object of the speaker. How largely does the expression of his eloquent countenance contribute to the impressiveness of his words ! Would it answer to interpose a screen of a thin board-partition between the preacher and his auditors ?

The crepuscular shadows of many places of worship have a not dissimilar effect. They seem to impair the sound of his voice; if not, they unquestionably diminish its effect. It is said that a man cannot detect the difference between wines of different sorts, if he tastes them in the darkness of a cellar. How then can he judge correctly of a sermon delivered in the dark? It has also been frequently asserted, and we believe with truth, that a smoker cannot tell, under the circumstances mentioned, whether the cigar in his mouth is really burning or not. It may be lighted, it may have gone out; he cannot tell.

We speak of *social* worship, as distinguished from solitary. We attribute to it valuable effects from the power of sympathy of heart with heart, mutually helping to kindle the flame of devotion. Yet what influence can an assembly of worshippers exercise over an individual, if that individual cannot see them?

Religion is not all darkness and sadness. It is also cheerful, bright, and hopeful. The heart requires such qualities, as well as others, in the object of reverence it loves to cling to. Thus the instincts of humanity prompted the disciples of Zoroaster and others to worship the sun, the fountain of light, joy, and hope. As far as worship can properly be made pleasant, that result should be thought of and secured. What possible good it does to put out the light of heaven in our places of worship, we are at a loss to discover. Some of the objections to it have been hinted. And if this were a proper subject to be tested by ridicule, it could be easily applied; for certainly it is laughable for a man to be spouting in a dark corner to a thousand invisible people, in an atmosphere such as bats and owls only prefer. If any reason exists for such a practice, it must be one discernible only by those lovers of night.

IN MEMORIAM.

"Mortales visus medio sermone reliquit."

October poured his yellow ray,
  The frost-stained leaf was hanging still;
Our thoughts were grave, our words not gay,
  For she who clasped my arm was ill.

Just then, we saw upon the right
  A field devoted to the dead.
It was abandoned, — hideous sight!
  Disgusting taste, inspiring dread.

A glance was all; she turned around,
  And, gazing sadly in my face,
Not there, she breathed, that trampled ground,
  Away from hence my body place.

Oh blessed health, without which all
  That we enjoy, or sigh for, dies, —
Why comes it at the wretch's call,
  And from the young and lovely flies?

Poor wand'rer for that priceless boon!
  Far from her kindred, country, friends,
Hope waves her on, but, ah! how soon
  The dream dissolves, and being ends.

The spring returned, and May once more
　Revived the pulses of the year,
That church-yard old, so grim before,
　Showed life and verdure even there.

Again the scene I lingered o'er,
　Where I had mused in autumn's pride;
All still was there I saw before,
　But where was she that graced my side?

Apart from men there smiles a spot,
　And heaven's own calm pervades the ground;
She there reposes, not forgot,
　The blue above, the green around!

But these are not the grass and sky
　Which on her native river shine;
The sleepers by her side that lie
　Did ne'er their hands with hers entwine.

Far to the east her kindred sleep,
　In seemly order, side by side;
Or live, the untimely fate to weep
　Of one who was their love and pride.

No matter, — 't is no matter where
　The wasted form shall spring to life;
With her let me be buried there,
　In death to slumber with that wife.

VALUE OF MONUMENTS.

MILLIONS upon millions have been lavished upon monuments, grand specimens of architecture, masterpieces in the fine arts, and works of skill and taste intended to give pleasure, but to yield no revenue. The propriety of consuming human industry and capital in such undertakings has been always questioned; they have always had defenders. Much may be said in vindication of their refining influence, their power to keep alive the sacred love of country, the flame of liberty, awaken the memory and provoke the emulation of noble deeds and public benefactors.

These are influences of great value, lofty, powerful, and pure in their effects. They have consequently been frequently urged in justification of great expenditures of money for what has been characterized as frivolous, useless, or ostentatious. We propose, however, now to pass all these considerations by, and measure their worth by their economical result in money. It will be embarrassing, we are aware, to prove the Pyramids a dividend-paying stock. Yet, putting them, the Obelisks, the Sphinx, Memnon, the Catacombs, with the ruins of the old cities on the Nile together, and saying nothing of the Cataracts, they must be admitted, one and all, to have caused foreign gold to be scattered over Egypt, though probably a small percentage upon the original investment in those works. The Pyramids must be allowed to be one of the very worst outlays of capital in existence; yet even that is not entirely dead.

None of these structures, however, can compare in point of a revenue-yielding work with the temple of St. Peter's. This, with the entertaining exhibitions there, looking on them with an eye to profit merely, and in a worldly point of view, must pay a handsome income on the first cost of the building, enormous as it was. Such expensive architecture cannot in conscience be recommended with a view of profits. Yet nothing is more certain than that such architectural wonders as this *chef-d'œuvre* of Buonarotti and the other great cathedrals and stupendous towers and monuments of the Old World, have not been money entirely thrown away, as generally represented. Nobody can tell the revenue they yield, paid voluntarily and silently by travellers. It is an unobserved but steady stream running into those countries which possess such works, and likely to augment from year to year, when the ease of communication offers an irresistible temptation for everybody to visit every place and gaze at everything.

As the gigantic works of man, erected apparently to gratify his pride, or the vanity of kings, nevertheless are followed by advantages of pecuniary profit to the countries which executed them, perhaps without any such expectation, other great works exist in which human ingenuity had no hand, that are such source of annual wealth. They cost the people nothing where they are, yet are the best property they have. What would Switzerland be without her mountains? The melting glaciers run down their sides under the summer sun. The world flocks thither to see it, while the coin in the pockets of the sight-seers dissolves in streams, and irrigates the whole territory which has the fortune to possess such fertilizers of her soil.

A report was current not long since, which has been recently revived, that some one had discovered a method by which Vesuvius could be prevented from making a periodic exhibition of itself. This would really be a monster project, worthy of the monster king of Naples; stupid because impracticable; more silly — were it not? — for it then would blow up the capital and himself. What do the fatuous of the Old World think they are visited for? Themselves? The last things a man of sense would

go a mile to see. A man travels to foreign lands
to see the reliques of former ages, what the people
of antiquity have left behind them, quite as much
as what their weak descendants are performing.
And, especially, men traverse inhospitable regions,
the more so sometimes the better, to witness nature
under strange aspects and in her most extraordinary
moods. Vesuvius, and what Vesuvius has done, are
among the principal treasures of that dark corner
of Italian despotism.

Deprive her of her museums, so richly filled with
the spoils of her burning mountain, — take away the
glorious skies which God has given her, the incom-
parable natural beauty of her land and air and water,
— and what will there then be for a traveller to
see? Nothing but an imbecile and inhuman Bour-
bon on the throne, and a beggarly people crouching
at its base. And, to keep to our pecuniary valuation
of the wonders of art and nature, his revenue would
soon proclaim the deprivation. Robbed of Vesuvius and other natural attractions, the foolish despot
would soon find out that he had lost the richest
jewels in his crown.

It is not only those who possess harbors, railroads,
and canals, that levy tolls upon the world, but they
who erect a column on Bunker Hill, to gaze upon;
a Broadway lined by stone and marble, to prome-
nade in; a gallery of pictures, or statues, to gratify

the taste, or a Park to regale the senses. The splendid residence and beautiful grounds of one man of elegant perceptions have been known to build up a town; and the cultivation and indulgence of similar dispositions on a larger scale made Athens what it was, Paris what it is, and will contribute, as well as the more gross calculations of trade, to advance the growth of New York, and expand its commerce. Enlightened men have known this always, and have therefore been, and still are, the advocates of the rising column, the massive church and its towering spire, the colossal pillar and fretted dome, the observatory and university. They are patrons of these, of course, on account of their appropriate design. To this we do not now refer. They are also favorable for their general attractions to travellers, to transient residents, to temporary and to permanent business. All these are attended with pecuniary emoluments, and go to create cities where they are not, and where they are, to convert them to emporiums.

CHRISTMAS.

OH, the merry, merry bells of Christmas! how they entwine themselves with the memories of our youthful days, when time had its quick-succeeding joys and sorrows, — seasons of happiness bubbling up and overflowing the full fountain of the heart; and then again seasons when it did not play any more than a New-York fountain, nor send up its sparkling jet of joy into the sunny sky, but all was sombre and overclouded. There were holidays and festivals, Saturday nights, moonlights, and sleigh-rides then, with the jingling bells. If the heart had its sorrow and dark passages, it had also its little streaks of sunlight streaming between the clouds; and life was not, as among the mature and advanced, a perpetual, dull, crepuscular shining through a hazy atmosphere, or a flat, straight turnpike-road, with neither turning, nor rise nor fall, nor shade-tree, nor pretty landscape on either side to entertain the traveller on his journey.

No matter though life be a checker-board, if, when one is passing over the black squares, the white ones

are only visible ahead, the passage will seem not
long, and the shadows of the dark will be relieved
by the light of the bright spots.   Beside, Youth has
this remarkable advantage: it neither anticipates nor
remembers evil and sorrow, while Age does both.
Look at the child: pain must be actually present to
make itself felt; and the joyous young thing is not
to be cheated of Heaven's gift of happiness by any
trick of the imagination, or by looking forward, or
backward, or one side or the other.   Superior to the
philosopher, it is no believer in abstract ideas, and is
therefore saved from the whole mischievous crew of
evils, that come in those disguises.   Youth is happy
when its senses are not pricked, and no tangible reason exists why it should not be so; while manhood
makes itself miserable, when it fails to prove itself
the contrary by a process of abstract reasoning.

Fortunate is the man who feels in his soul when
Christmas has come, and has not lost his relish for
the simple festival seasons of the calendar.   It is
well to be resolute in business, to be ambitious of
honest fame, and even for some persons to be absorbed in the giant task of saving their country.
But for most of us, a corner of the heart had better
be reserved for the residence of quiet thoughts
and satisfaction amid the desperate struggles of the
world.   It is best for one to snatch as much enjoyment as he can, from the floods or fires that are

burning up or drowning human hopes all around him. We will resolve not to lose, if we can help it, a single one of the games and gayeties, freaks and follies of Christmas eve, or morn, or noon, or night. We will not let one stick fall out of the fagot in which, on Christmas, delights are bound up, and which makes the blessed Nativity what it is, and has been, immemorially away back in the dim days of the distant past. We will not forget to be happy ourselves, as some do, when the time for it, long anticipated, actually arrives.

But that must not be all. We must remember to make others happy also, if in our power, once at least a year, and that at Christmas, and as much oftener as we are able. But when Christmas comes, let everybody around us know it, — those under our roof, those in our neighborhood. Let us prove that our Saviour did not die for nought; but that his shed blood has been converted to a stream of charity to the destitute, and consolation to the unhappy. What! shut up the heart at such a blessed season! Our inclement climate compels the closing of doors; otherwise they should all stand open, and every household should be free to all as Heaven's common on that day.

The first of the year is a meagre shadow and imitation in this respect of what Christmas ought to be in substance. The coffers of the rich are running over; why not let the poor hold their empty cups to catch the overflow? The bags of grain are bursting in the corn-house; there are deserving people enough who will be glad to stop the leak and prevent the loss. No need that fruits should rot in the bins or barrels, or coats be devoured by the moths. Christmas is a remedy for all this mischief, and mouths and backs enough are open and ready to save them all from ruin. Heaven provides enough, in the worst of times, to satisfy all its children, if the fences, obstacles, and tricks of men did not hinder it from reaching the needy consumer. For the selfish and unbrotherly contrivances to tax the poor, the hard, unsympathizing possessors of property sustain losses which would be very near sufficient for their reasonable desires.

And Christmas is a powerful preacher of gratitude for the Evangel, Heaven's best gift to man, and of the charities and kindnesses of life, as well as the fomenter of a host of frolicsome humors. St. Nicholas, the children's benefactor, who, good fellow as he is, is bountiful by stealth, and takes as much pains to avoid notice as other people do to purchase it, — this patron of little folks takes the eve of Christmas to revisit the earth, and scatter his comical gifts, like the night dew, all over the land. Oh, the merry, merry bells of Christmas! Well have good spirits been imagined to tenant them, with power to chase away all evil ones from the neighborhood with their sweet and holy melodies. As thus animated, they have received the rites of baptism from the Church, and borne upon their brazen fronts divers wild or sacred inscriptions; one of which is just at hand in the recent " Golden Legend " of Longfellow, which runs as follows : —

<table>
<tr><td>" Laudo Deum verum !</td><td>Funera plango!</td></tr>
<tr><td>Plebem voco!</td><td>Fulgora frango!</td></tr>
<tr><td>Congrego clerum!</td><td>Sabbata pango! "</td></tr>
</table>

The same beautiful poem has the following on bells : —

" For the bells themselves are the best of preachers:
　Their brazen lips are learnèd teachers,
　From their pulpits of stone, in the upper air,
　Sounding aloft, without crack or flaw,
　Shriller than trumpets under the Law,
　Now a sermon and now a prayer.
　The clangorous hammer is the tongue,
　This way, that way, beaten and swung,
　That from mouth of brass, as from mouth of gold,
　May be taught the Testaments, New and Old.
　And above it the great cross-beam of wood
　Representeth the Holy Rood,
　Upon which, like the bell, our hopes are hung.
　And the wheel wherewith it is swayed and rung
　Is the mind of man, that round and round
　Sways, and maketh the tongue to sound ! "

Chime on, ye Christmas bells, and bear on your silvery waves the good news of the Evangel. The people will pause to listen to the unusual annunciation from their ponderous tongues, — " Peace on earth and good-will among men."

THE BURIAL.

Make way! make way! for the prostrate dead!
She leaves forever her long-prest bed,
To make her couch in the dark cold tomb;
Make room for the dead to pass! make room!

She stays not for darkness, cold, nor storm;
The crowd gives way to the lifeless form;
The steamer awaits the silent freight,
For Death goes free, and is never late!

Away! away! o'er the sullen tide!
On its restless bosom she may not bide.
Blow high, ye winds, and thunders roar!
She hears your rattling blast no more.

No pause, no rest, for that lonely one,
Where the life-pulse beats, where shines the sun.
On! onward she hastes through the ranks of men,
As the cloud's black shade cuts the sunlit plain.

The journey is closed. Here the cypress keeps
Its solemn watch, and the willow weeps.
The village kindred repose below;
Above waves the grass, and flowers blow.

Now, fare thee well, thou much-loved clay!
We must leave thee here with the worm to-day.
No, no, my soul; be not thus cast down!
Look up! for thither thy friend has gone!

THE WANING YEAR.

TIME — Time — Time is — what? He is "the oldest inhabitant" of this rather dingy island of ours, dashed up by the collision of two great oceans, — the infinite Past and the infinite Future. He lives in the sparkling white momentary ripples, which, like little children's feet, run upon the smooth, sandy beach, when the tide is flowing in, and then run back again to sink forever in the dark, illimitable sea. Time is somebody in the old family-clock that is saying, tick, tick, tick, all day long, and is busy at the same work also the lifelong night, when one is lying awake, and watching for Christmas or New-Year's coming, or thinking of a dear child or friend who is no more. I remember to have heard the same stroke at that still and awful moment when my father died. It sounded very loud then to my ear, and struck directly on my heart. A parent holds down his great gold watch to the ear of his wondering boy, and tells him that the mysterious noise within comes from a little fellow cutting wood, — pleasanter intelligence than to inform him truly, that it is made by old Time, whetting his remorseless scythe, so sharp already, to cut in two the stripling's thread of life.

But the singular individual we call Time is not always engaged in occupations such as these, and in climbing up into great church-steeples, to chime out the solitary hours, as they are born into existence and die away again along the old mouldy tombs, which darken and consecrate their long shadows. He can move about as deftly as a cat at a mouse-hole, or as gingerly as a doctor in the perfumed chamber of a wealthy invalid. Nobody sees him do it, yet he is softly planting indubitable wrinkles continually in the prettiest of faces, and gets from his furrow exceeding good crops, too, in a few brief years. The premonitory and alarming crow's-feet in reality are nothing but his footprints. There is not a barber among them all who is his match "for thinning our flowing hair," and powdering it with the salt that is destined to preserve it in the grave, long after we have done with it ourselves.

To do him justice, however, he is not always, it must be owned, employed in mischief. He also causes the young moustache to bud, swells into fair proportions the maiden's ductile limbs, clothes her cheek with vermilion down, richer than the peach-bloom, and weaves her curling tresses into " springes to catch woodcocks."

Yet more. When bereavement has torn our hearts, and affliction planted in the memory a rooted sorrow which medicine is unable to pluck out, there Time, the good physician, humanely hastens, though unsent for, to pour upon the wound the oblivion-drop we all require in turn, for we are human,

> —— " and must feel calamity as men ;
> We cannot but remember such things were,
> That were most precious to us."

On such occasions Time calmly and kindly interposes his dusky wing between us and the past, screens it from the sight, and thus softens for us the bitterest sorrows.

He is ever bringing sad changes upon people with more or less rapidity, though oftentimes as slow as the hour-hand of a clock in sermon-time. All wax old sufficiently fast no doubt, yet, while one is looking at it, he is scarcely able to discern the almost imperceptible shadow creeping over the familiar countenance, and dimming the lustre of its beauty. But let an interval pass by, and look again! A portion of its original brightness has departed, and can never be relit. Notwithstanding an occasional apparent pause, yet, on the whole, Time is a swift traveller. Steam and the telegraph are added to our ancient velocities, and still it can be affirmed with emphasis that Time flies ! His speed is, after all, unmatched, for he posts from this world to the next — a fearful distance — in the twinkling of an eye, and carries us with him in his car.

There is a period in life when Time appears to be almost standing still. That period is youth. Looking forward, as the young do, to future objects in long perspective, Time seems as motionless to them as a distant waterfall. They grow older, and, on approaching, find their error. Soon, however, an opposite one occurs. Old age arrives, and the senses become so bewildered with the extreme rapidity of the fleeting moments, that, sometimes, like physical bodies moving with immense velocity through space, they overtask the faculty of appreciation, and become invisible. To the aged, " the present " is nothing, and " we live " becomes an expression in the past tense.

Time — Time — Time is — where ? He is in the flower-garden, pulling open with subtle fingers the petals of a rose-bud on a summer morning. He is in the woodlands, raining down the decaying foliage of the aged chestnut in the autumn. He is omnipresent: at the self-same moment undermining the venerable monarch of the forest and the thrones of the Bourbons and Hapsburgs; covering over and obliterating with the brown moss of the churchyard the memorials on the head-stones of the dead; and, responsively to the solemn voices of the old clock in the corner, " beating funeral-marches to the tomb " within the bosoms of all the living. Listen! Hear his hollow voice within and around us, saying, as the clock says at every dull swing of the pendulum, — " Prepare, prepare!" It is a startling thing, sometimes, to hear the old time-piece speaking after its maker is in the grave. This monition is all that Time can utter; a voice of warning is his no more. A passage across the domain of life he secures us, but at its confines his journey with us ends, and we must afterwards go on alone. If we have taken care to have our passports duly *viséd* before quitting his dominions, it will be well.

REBELLION AGAINST A FREE GOVERN-MENT.

Oppressed with years, and blind,
I still could bear these; but my mind
Is doomed a heavier grief to feel, —
My country drenched in gore from her own children's steel.

Most beautiful of earth !
Land of my ripest choice, and birth,
How can my heart be ever false to thee,
Who bearest a mother's love — and only love — to me ?

The worm spares not the tree
Whence he derives vitality;
The beast will turn and rend, in mutual strife,
The parent-brute from which he drew the stream of life :

But man, of spirit sprung,
The first God's visible works among,
When grown a traitor, sinks below them all,
And, basest of the base, can never deeper fall.

I 've searched through every age,
And found on history's blood-red page
That Treason is of blackest crimes the worst,
By Heaven detested, and by all mankind accursed.

And must I sit and sigh,
Nor strike one blow for Liberty,
While Rebel hands are tearing down the fane,
Which, once demolished here, may never rise again ?

List ! list ! cheer up, my soul !
Away the Rebel squadrons roll ;
The distant thunder of their hoofs I hear, —
Sweet music ringing to a weary loyal ear.

The cannon's awful roar
Shall shake and terrify no more.
On the battlefield, where strong men fought and fell,
The timid flower shall spring and spread its spicy spell.

My country ! sweetest name !
Henceforth I 've given thee up to fame ;
Rebellion vanquished, Freedom looked and smiled,
Fair Liberty and thou, — the Mother and the Child.

Our Western Paradise,
Of serpent-treason purged, shall rise ;
Serene in Union, she shall fear no harm,
From enemies intestine, or from foreign arm.

'T will not be mine to see
My country's coming destiny ;
Then some young Milton's muse sublime shall tell
Where streamed the patriot flag, where the Rebel banner fell.

This only may I say,
That none again shall see the day
When man shall dare his brother's blood to draw,
To curse mankind with slave rebellion or slave law.

FAREWELL.

THE girls have been all the forenoon packing their huge trunks; and now the labor is ended, and the order is given, " John, strap your mistresses' baggage, and bring it down into the hall to be ready for the carriage at three o'clock." A depressing sight, those corpulent trunks, deposited side by side. Painful associations are awakened by some of them. They have a history; the Past is disinterred, and contrasts dimly and disagreeably with the Present, like candles burning in the sunshine, and a transient faintness passes through the frame. Reassured, we are standing next upon the pier. The brave steamer, like a racer, impatient for the start, feels the strong impulse of internal fire and life, and seems clamorous at delay. Mary and Charlotte are on board; the parting kiss has been given; a " God be with you " breathed; and the last farewell but half whispered, for the choking throat refused to utter it.

Alas ! alas ! how much unhappiness is bound up in that soft word, farewell ! We are aware it is sometimes uttered lightly. To us it ever has a tone of melancholy, — sometimes almost of sorrow, and even despair. It can never again become a common word to us ; for we have known it hallowed by quick-following suffering and death. It flows trippingly from the lips of the vigorous and young, upon a supposed temporary parting ; but it has, in such cases, often proved a last, long farewell, never to be repeated, never to be forgotten. How many such solemn last words are interchanged with friends at this season of the year, when multitudes are gayly planning separations, little dreaming they are to be eternal !

It is indeed a serious thing to part, even for a night ; and many never omit those touching customs which presuppose and provide for the sudden, perhaps instantaneous, occurrence of the greatest of events. In such an evanescent state, shall individuals and families thoughtlessly, and without the least good reason, plunge blindly into the hazards of an everlasting separation from their friends ? If modern improvements have almost repealed the laws of nature, they have not, as we fondly hope, quite done away with those of the affections, though we fear they have materially impaired their tenderness and force.

But the boasted advancement of human skill and power is still limited indeed, and has scarcely touched at all the two grand phenomena of life and death. Man is just as mortal as he ever was, and has little more control than formerly of his ebbing sands. The sober word *farewell* has lost nothing of its sadness. Though it has rung so long and often in our ears, we still wait with tearful eyes yet perhaps smiling lips, while they drink in these mournful syllables as greedily as ever, and convey them directly to the heart. It is a word which can never be vulgarized by use. On the contrary, it acquires a more significant meaning and a higher sanctity from year to year. The associations of the departed cluster round it, as being the final word which passed between the living and the dying. At moments, particularly when the heart is softened by misfortune, mortality, or the separation of families or friends for considerable periods, the affectionate accents of the old familiar term, *farewell*, have a magic potency in peopling the soul with memories of the departed, the absent, and the dead, connected with anxious misgivings and monitions in relation to the present and the living.

Chastised, if not subdued, by tender sentiments like these, I now bid *Adieu*, perhaps forever, to the few or many who have done me the honor of giving me their company, and listening to any portion of the reflections contained in the preceding pages.

THE END.